Best Friends Forever?

Renée Kent

ADVENTURES IN MISTY FALLS

2

Best Friends Forever?

Renée Kent

New Hope® Publishers

Birmingham, Alabama

New Hope® Publishers
P.O. Box 12065
Birmingham, AL 35202-2065
www.newhopepubl.com

Library of Congress Cataloging-in-Publication Data

Kent, Renee Holmes, 1955-
  Best friends forever? / Renee Kent.
      p. cm. -- (Adventures in Misty Falls ; bk. 2)
Summary: When Cassie fears that the presence of a new girl may change her relationship with her best friend, she learns to share her love as Jesus does.
  ISBN 1-56309-734-6
  [1. Best friends--Fiction.
  2. Christian life--Fiction.]
  I. Title.   PZ7.K419 Be 2000
  [Fic]--dc21   99-050713

Cover design by Todd Cotton
Cover illustration by Matt Archambault

ISBN: 1-56309-734-6
N007117 • 1202 • 1.5M2

Misty Falls, Georgia

Best Friends Forever?

1

"Oomph!" said Cassie Holbrook as she lifted a large covered box of Snickerdoodles out of the back seat of the car with great effort. Her best friend, J.J. Graystone, lifted the other extra big box of cookies.

"Hey Cassie, the bottom of that box is going to break open," warned Iggy Potts. "You'd better support it underneath."

"Looks like you could help us a little," said Cassie, straining under the awkward load.

As usual, their pal Iggy took pictures of them with his camera. "Okay," said Iggy. "I'll help." With one hand he held the camera, snapping photos. With the other hand, he opened the door of the Misty Falls Community Church for them.

"Gee, thanks." Cassie said with a giggle.

The delicious smell of homemade soup greeted their noses as they walked toward the church kitchen. Cassie tried to shift the weight of the bulky box so her hands wouldn't ache quite so much. By the time they arrived in the shiny-clean kitchen, the box felt twice as heavy. She almost couldn't lift it onto the table.

"Whew!" puffed J.J. "I never knew cookies could weigh so much!"

"Me either," agreed Cassie as she wrung her hands to make them feel better.

"Maybe you baked too many stinky poodles," said Iggy, teasing.

Cassie rolled her hazel eyes. Sometimes Iggy could go just a little too far. She patted the top of her big box and sternly scolded him.

"Now listen, Iggy Potts, don't start that again. For the last time, these cookies are not stinky poodles. They are Snickerdoodles. Case closed!"

Iggy faked a hurt look. The freckles on his forehead squished together. "You don't have to get all cranky about it," he said, trying to pout. But the corners of his mouth curled into a smile.

J.J. giggled and winked at Cassie. The bright yellow and red beads in her hair clicked together, as J.J. swept her long, dark hair away from her face. She opened the door of the kitchen and peeked out.

"Uh-oh," she said. "It looks like we are going to need all these cookies—maybe even more!"

"Let me see," said Iggy. His fire-red, curly hair tick-led Cassie's nose as he pushed past her. He tugged at J.J. until she moved out of the way. Then he poked out his freckled face to sneak a peek.

Best Friends Forever?

Cassie stood on tiptoe and looked over Iggy's shoulder into the brightly lit room. "Wow!" was all she could say.

On one end of the dining hall were cots and chairs. Nurses were already busy. A lady on one cot rolled up her sleeve and held out her arm for the nurse. She seemed happy to give a pint of blood for hospital patients who might need it to get well.

People were beginning to form a line at the nurse's registration desk, which was near the door. More and more men and women began to pour into the Misty Falls Community Church dining hall, even though it was very early in the morning. Pretty soon the line began to look like one extra-long spaghetti noodle, winding around the sides of the room.

"How are we going to feed all these people?" asked Cassie.

"I don't know," said J.J. with a shrug.

"Hello!" A lady's cheerful voice behind them startled Cassie, J.J., and Iggy. All three jumped with surprise.

Cassie's light auburn ponytail swung about as she turned to see who was speaking to them.

"Oh, Mrs. Reed," she said with a big smile. It was the nice judge from the Misty Falls Fair who had asked Cassie to bake the cookies for the people at the blood drive.

"Oh my," said Mrs. Reed, gazing at the two large boxes of cookies. "You really have been busy!

Everyone will enjoy your Snickerdoodles today, Cassie. Thank you for helping to make our annual blood drive a big success."

"J.J. helped me bake them," said Cassie. "We thought we'd never finish! But I promised you oodles and oodles of Snickerdoodles, and here they are!"

Mrs. Reed laughed good-heartedly. "I'm sure everyone will enjoy them," she said, smoothing her green-checked apron. "Here, let's place some cookies on these serving trays and get the punch ready."

Cassie and J.J. began to put dozens of cookies onto the serving trays while Iggy took photos of them. Suddenly he paused. He scratched his chin and scrunched up his nose. "Boy, I hope those stinky poodles taste better today than they did at the fair," he said.

Cassie shot him a warning look, but she couldn't help laughing. That was Iggy—not a serious bone in his body. Cassie didn't *really* mind his teasing because they had been friends for such a long time. Besides, she knew how much he liked to eat her homemade cookies.

The expression on Iggy's face changed to a look of confusion. "Hey, why did you want us to bring cookies today anyway?" He asked.

Mrs. Reed responded cheerfully. "The people who give some of their blood today for the hospital will eat a bowl of soup and the cookies. Providing food is a way of saying 'thank you' for donating blood."

"Yes," said J.J. "Donating blood helps lots of hospital patients get well."

"Oh," said Iggy.

"Also," added Mrs. Reed, "the sugar in the cookies will help the people who share their blood feel stronger as they leave to go back to work, school, or home."

Iggy swallowed hard. "Yicch. Talking about cookies and blood doesn't seem to go together very well. I don't like the word 'blood.' It's creepy."

J.J. laughed. "Don't look at the blood in the little bags, then. Maybe you should stick to taking pictures," she teased.

Which is just what Iggy did. He disappeared into the big room with a pocket full of extra film and the viewfinder on his camera pressed against his eye. People in line smiled at him as he took their pictures. The nice nurse at the registration table made a funny face at Iggy as the camera flash went off.

Meanwhile, Cassie and J.J. got very busy in the kitchen. They made enough punch to fill Possum Creek. Just as the girls finished stirring gallons and gallons of pink punch, Mrs. Reed announced, "Alright! It's time to serve the multitude."

"What's a multitude?" whispered J.J. But there was no time for Cassie to reply.

J.J. and Cassie had never smiled so much and served so many cookies in their lives. Halfway through the morning, Cassie's feet began to tingle. She wished she had worn more comfortable shoes! All the trips of scurrying to and from the kitchen for more cookies, punch, or Mrs. Reed's vegetable soup were starting to make her feet hurt. But there wasn't much time to think about her achy feet.

"And how old are you, young lady?" asked an attractive woman in a blue business suit.

"Eleven," said Cassie, adding quickly, "but I'll be twelve in November. Would you like some cookies and punch or soup?"

The woman glanced at her watch. "I do have a few minutes before my next meeting," she said. "Thank you!" Taking a bite, she exclaimed, "Mmm, these are delicious. Perhaps I'll take one more."

"I'm glad you like them," said Cassie proudly.

The girls were so busy that they had lost track of Iggy. "Where is he?" J.J. whispered to Cassie. "Do you think he left?"

"Oh there he is—way over there in the corner," said Cassie. "I should have known. He's still looking through that camera lens."

The girls chuckled as Iggy snapped photographs of a man who was donating a pint of blood. The man pleasantly chatted with the nurse and smiled for the camera.

But suddenly Iggy didn't look so well. As Cassie continued to serve cookies, she observed the strange look on Iggy's face. When he lowered the camera from his face, it was plain to see that even his freckles had turned a pale shade of green. With his curly red hair, he resembled an old, faded Christmas decoration.

Cassie felt a little concerned. "J.J., look at Iggy. Do you think he's okay? Come on, we'd better check on him."

The girls didn't even take time to put down their trays of cookies. They hurried over to Iggy with refreshments in hand. As the nurse threw away a long needle and pulled off her latex gloves, the man sat up and asked, "Are we finished already? That didn't take long."

"Just rest for a few minutes, Mr. Phillips," said the nurse, smiling. "Oh look, the girls have some punch and cookies for you."

"Thank you, young ladies," said Mr. Phillips. He glanced at Iggy and smiled. "It's nice to be photographed and waited on hand and foot. I've never felt so appreciated before."

"Did it hurt, Mister?" asked Iggy, turning greener. It seemed like Iggy's tongue wasn't working very well, as he tried to form the words.

"Oh not at all," Mr. Phillips replied. "I give blood twice a year. And don't worry, there's still plenty of blood left to take care of my own body."

Iggy smiled weakly. "Say, Nurse, uh, what are you going to do with all the blood in those little bags?"

"Call me Trixie," she said with a broad smile. Then she added, "The blood will be stored in our blood bank."

Iggy took an uneasy deep breath. "That's weird. I only put money in the bank."

The girls giggled. "No, silly," said Cassie. "The blood bank is a refrigerated storage area at the hospital."

"That's right," said Nurse Trixie. "We keep the blood frozen in these little bags until very sick patients need it to get well."

"Oh," said Iggy unsteadily. "I knew that." He swallowed hard over and over and wiped his sweaty forehead. "Boy, is it getting hot in here?"

"What's the matter, Iggy? Feeling weak in the knees?" J.J. teased.

Just then, Iggy's eyes began to flutter, and his body began to sway. Cassie moved slowly toward him and then rushed to catch him. "Iggy? Nurse Trixie! Help!"

But it was too late. Iggy had fainted.

Best Friends Forever?

2

Nurse Trixie managed to catch Iggy as he went limp. She gently eased him into a nearby chair as Cassie patted his pale cheeks.

"Wow, that was close," said J.J. "I'm glad a trained nurse was standing right here."

Cassie felt a little sorry about teasing Iggy. "What's wrong with him?" she asked.

Trixie said, "Don't worry. This will wake him up." She waved a small, smelly cotton ball in front of Iggy's nose. "Some people get a little light-headed at the sight of blood. I suppose Iggy is one of those people. He will feel much better in a moment."

Just then, Iggy lifted his head and looked at Nurse Trixie, then J.J., and then Cassie. His eyes seemed disconnected from each other. They sort of rolled around in wobbly circles.

"What happened?" he asked in a foggy sort of way.

"You fainted, but you're going to be fine now," Trixie comforted him.

"I did? I fainted? I really fainted? Cool!" said Iggy, his eyes widening with wonder. "Wow! Cassie, quick! Take my picture!"

Cassie snorted. "Oh Iggy, I don't think now is a good time for a picture. You're as green as a cucumber. Why don't you just relax until you feel better?"

"I feel fine now," he said, trying to stand. "Hey, my legs won't work! They feel squiggly like jelly."

"Squiggly Iggy," J.J. whispered softly. Then the girls burst into nervous giggles.

The nurse placed her hands firmly on Iggy's shoulders. "I suggest you just sit here for a few more minutes, young man. Would one of you girls bring Iggy a fresh cup of punch?"

Cassie and J.J. both scurried to the serving table. J.J. held a cup while Cassie poured, and they walked quickly back to Iggy's side. They watched as he took small, shaky sips.

In a bit, some pink color returned to Iggy's freckles. Then he finished off the cupful in big gulps. "That's good stuff. Thanks," he said sheepishly.

Now was the time to lighten the mood. Cassie tweaked his arm.

"Silly old Iggy! Funny that you fainted, and you didn't even give blood," she said.

Best Friends Forever?

"I bet it's easier to give blood than to watch!" he said defensively.

Nurse Trixie laughed loudly and said, "You're probably right, Iggy. I have been giving blood every few months to the hospital blood bank, and it has never bothered me. But when I was in nursing school, I had to learn how to take blood properly from patients. I became queasy at times. It took practice, but it doesn't bother me now."

Deep in thought, J.J. brushed her long dark hair away from her golden-brown face. Her dark, indigo eyes seemed even darker than usual.

"It is scary to be a patient in the hospital and need someone else's blood to live," she said.

"What? How do you know?" asked Cassie, puzzled.

"When I was four years old and lived on the Navajo reservation in Arizona, my appendix burst," said J.J. "After the operation, the doctors told my family that I had lost a lot of blood. They said the blood in the blood bank saved my life."

Cassie shivered as she responded, "Oh J.J., you never told me that!" She couldn't imagine life without Jennifer Joy Graystone, her very best friend in the whole world.

J.J. and Cassie had known each other ever since first grade when J.J. moved to Misty Falls with her mother. Since then, they had been through everything together—from losing baby teeth and growing new, bigger ones to the time when J.J.'s parents' divorce became final last year.

"I'm glad the blood bank was there when you needed it," Cassie added, hugging J.J.

Nurse Trixie smiled at them. "It's plain to see that you three are good friends."

"Best friends," said Cassie cheerfully. She tossed her light auburn ponytail and accidentally pelted J.J. in the nose. Of course, Iggy captured the funny moment on film.

"I know some children about your age at the reha-bilitation center where I work," said Trixie.

"What in the world is a ree-ha-billy-station center?" asked Iggy, scrunching his nose in a way that only Iggy could do.

"That's re-ha-bil-it-ay-shun," said Nurse Trixie, trying to hide her amusement.

"Don't even try to help him pronounce it," giggled Cassie. "He still can't say 'Snickerdoodles'."

"I can too say stinky poodles, I mean sneaky noo-dles. Oh, never mind!" said Iggy. "So what is that, you know, that center where you work, Nurse Trixie?"

"Don't worry, Iggy. There's another name for where I work, and it's a name you can pronounce. It's the New Hope Center."

"Why didn't you say that in the first place?" said Iggy, teasingly. "I can say New Hope Center ten times fast with a mouth full of bubble gum."

Best Friends Forever?

Cassie shook her head. "Never mind him, Nurse Trixie. Is New Hope Center like a hospital?"

"Not exactly," Trixie explained. "When children are released from the hospital, they usually get to go home. But if they need a lot of physical therapy and medical attention, they come to our center to continue getting well. The New Hope Center feels a little more like home than a hospital."

"Are they our age?" asked J.J.

"Oh yes, and some are younger or older too," said Trixie. "There is one young lady who has spent most of her life in and out of hospitals. She is as cheerful as a little bird, though. I could introduce you. Would you kids like to visit New Hope Center?"

"Sure!" exclaimed J.J. as she exchanged a hopeful glance with Cassie.

Even though Cassie felt a little shy about meeting new people, she wanted to visit the New Hope Center. It sounded like fun, especially since her best friends would be with her. Besides, now that the fair was over, there wouldn't be much left to do this summer until school started.

"Can I bring my camera?" asked Iggy hopefully.

"I think that can be arranged," said Nurse Trixie with an amused grin.

Cassie giggled. "It's a good thing he can bring his camera. He always has it stuck to his eyeballs. I think it sprouted roots and is growing to his head!"

Everyone chuckled as Iggy blushed as red as his hair. Nurse Trixie assured him. "The children would enjoy posing for photographs. We could make a cheerful bulletin board display."

"When can we come?" asked J.J. eagerly.

Nurse Trixie gave them details about visiting hours at New Hope Center. Now all they had to do was get permission from their parents and go!

Best Friends Forever?

3

Late that same afternoon, Cassie, J.J., and Iggy burst into Cassie's house. They found her mom folding laundry in the family room.

"Oh good," Mrs. Holbrook said. "You're home in time to help me fold all these T-shirts."

"What fun," Cassie teased. But she really didn't mind. Even Iggy and J.J. joined in. It was the first T-shirt-folding party they had ever attended. There were certainly a lot of T-shirts to fold. Some belonged to Cassie, but most of them belonged to other members of the family—Cassie's sisters' cheerleading camp T-shirts, Dad's faded farming T-shirts that he liked to work in on hot summer days, and Cassie's brother Jeff's varsity football camp shirts.

"So," said Mrs. Holbrook, making a stack in the laundry basket, "Mrs. Reed just called a few minutes ago to tell me what a big help you were today. It sounds like the blood drive was very successful."

"Except for one thing," said Iggy, sounding mysterious.

"Oh? What's that?" asked Mrs. Holbrook.

"I fainted," answered Iggy.

"Oh my," said Mrs. Holbrook, looking concerned. "Are you alright?"

"Yeah," laughed Iggy, "I must have eaten too many stinky poodles."

Cassie threw one of her dad's T-shirts at Iggy, while J.J. giggled. "Never mind him," said Cassie. "Mrs. Reed said it was the best blood drive that Misty Falls has ever had."

"That's wonderful!" exclaimed Mrs. Holbrook.

"Yes," said J.J. "And when the last person left, we had three Snickerdoodles left."

"Is that all?" asked Mother. "And where are those three leftover cookies?"

"I ate them," said Iggy.

"Well frankly," said Mrs. Holbrook, "I'm quite happy that the cookie baking is over for a while. But what will you all do with your time now that the fair and the blood drive are both over? I'm afraid the rest of the summer will be quite boring for you."

As Cassie stacked her freshly folded laundry, she asked, "Mom, have you ever heard of the New Hope Center?"

"Oh, the rehabilitation center in the southern section of the county," said Mother. "Yes, I've driven past there a few times on my way to Atlanta. Why do you ask?"

"Can you take us there?" blurted out Iggy. "Nurse Trixie invited us."

"Wait, wait, wait," said Mrs. Holbrook. "Who in the world is Nurse Trixie?"

Suddenly, Cassie, J.J., and Iggy were bubbling with news. They each tried to take turns explaining to Cassie's mom about Nurse Trixie and the recovery center for ill children, until finally she understood the whole story.

"So you children want to ride out to the New Hope Center for a visit. I think it's a wonderful idea! I'll drive you out there Saturday."

"Great!" said J.J. "Thank you, Mrs. Holbrook. Oh, but I guess I still need to talk to my mom. I think she might have plans to take me with her to the children's museum where she works. But I would rather go to New Hope Center."

"Oh, yeah," said Iggy, his smile fading. "I promised my dad I would help him run the photography shop this Saturday. I wonder if he will let me off for a few hours?"

The children looked at each other quietly and then up at Mrs. Holbrook. They knew that getting permission from Iggy's father and J.J.'s mother and arranging a visit to New Hope Center would take some fancy footwork. That's what Cassie's mother always said when complicated plans had to be made. But Mrs. Holbrook was a big help.

She even contacted J.J.'s mom and Iggy's parents and committed to take the trio to New Hope Center Saturday afternoon. It was no surprise to Cassie that her mother was so willing to help them arrange their visit. After all, her mom was like a missionary at heart. She was always thinking up ways for her daughter to help people (whether Cassie wanted to or not!).

Finally, the short trip to New Hope Center was all set for Saturday at 2:00 P.M. Mrs. Holbrook even invited J.J. to spend the night with Cassie on Saturday.

Cassie hugged her mom and whispered, "May she stay tonight too?"

"Yes…that is, of course," paused Mrs. Holbrook, "if you put away your laundry."

The girls hopped up and down and squealed with delight as Iggy rolled his eyes. "I'm sure glad I'm not a girl," he said.

"We're glad you're not a girl, too," teased Cassie, as she and J.J. exchanged grins. They each gripped a handle on either side of the laundry basket and proceeded up the stairs to put the clothes away.

When they finished with the chore, the three ran out the door into the sunshine. Across the field, they ran into the old barn. The sun beamed through large slits between the boards in the walls. Iggy looked up at the old, worn out basketball goal that Cassie's dad had

Best Friends Forever?

nailed up for the boys when Cassie was very young. His eyes twinkled with mischief.

"I challenge you two to a basketball tournament," said Iggy.

"You're on," said Cassie, winking at J.J. Pretty soon, they were into a heated game of basketball inside the old barn—two girls against one Iggy.

Across the hard-packed dirt floor, the three friends dribbled the ball.

Back and forth, their shadows danced against the rickety walls of the old barn. Iggy was a little taller than the girls, giving him the advantage. Still, J.J. could sneak around Iggy for lay-up shots while Cassie distracted him. Because of playing hundreds of games with her older brothers Sid and Jeff, Cassie could shoot accurately if she was within four feet of the hoop. Soon Iggy was growing dizzy from his tag team opponents.

As Cassie's final shot circled around the rim three times and slipped through the hoop, the girls whooped and jumped up and down.

"We won!" said J.J., giving her teammate a high five.

"Na-ah," said Iggy. "That last shot didn't count. Cassie had one foot out of bounds."

Cassie shook her head and laughed. "Oh Iggy, you just can't stand to lose. I was nowhere near the line. See? There's my footprint in the dirt," she remarked. They all examined the spot. Sure enough, the footprint was a good six inches away from the boundary line.

"Aww, I just let you win," teased Iggy. "Besides, that was just the first game of the tournament."

They all came out of the barn, smiling sweaty smiles. To their surprise, Mr. Potts' car was in the driveway. They hadn't even heard Iggy's dad drive up the Holbrooks' lane!

Iggy looked exactly like his father. They were both tall and slim with curly red hair and eyelashes. But the elder Mr. Potts was growing a small bald spot in the crown of his head.

Mr. Potts was on the front porch talking with Cassie's parents as the three approached.

"Well, kids," said Mr. Potts, aiming Iggy's camera at Iggy, J.J., and Cassie, "it looks like you all could use a bath."

Iggy examined himself and said, "Oh, Pop, its just a little barn dust." He brushed himself off. "See? Good as new!"

"We beat him," said Cassie, poking Iggy with her elbow.

The adults chuckled as Mr. Potts and Iggy headed toward the car. "Maybe I'll see you tomorrow," called Iggy, waving to the girls.

As the Potts drove away, Cassie and J.J. waved good-bye. Then they dashed to the new barn to look in on Chester. Mr. Holbrook had built it last year. It still had that "new" smell to it, mixed with the fragrances of hay, grain, and leather. Chester was the fattest pony in Misty Falls. Still, he was always hungry and ready to eat.

When Cassie and J.J. entered the barn, Chester peeked over the top of his stall with his ears perked high. He nuzzled Cassie's shirt pocket for a sweet apple but found nothing. Disappointed, he snorted and nuzzled Cassie's face as if to beg, "Please! Just a nibble!"

"Oh, no you don't," said Cassie, pushing his nose away. "You need to work off that round belly. You're taking us for a ride, boy."

The girls gave Chester's spotted coat a vigorous brushing and slipped on his bridle. Cassie went to get the saddle, but J.J. said, "Let's ride him bareback!"

Cassie dropped the saddle in the dust. "You're kidding, aren't you?" she wailed. "I need a saddle horn to hold onto."

J.J. smiled softly. "You can hold onto me! I'll ride in front, and you ride in back. It will be fun!" she said excitedly.

Cassie wasn't so sure about this. But since J.J. was such an experienced rider, she felt a little better. Besides, it would be an adventure, and Cassie couldn't resist an adventure, especially with her very best friend in the whole world.

With great ease, J.J. took a running start and slipped onto Chester's back. She gathered up the reins and looked at Cassie. "Okay, your turn. Come on up," said J.J.

Cassie had never tried to climb onto a horse without a saddle and stirrups. She just stared at J.J. in amazement. "How did you get up there?" she asked.

J.J. giggled. "I just ran and hopped," she said.

"Hopped?" asked Cassie. "I can't hop that high."

"Sure you can," said J.J. "Go ahead. I'll hold Chester real steady."

Cassie felt very doubtful. But it was worth a try. She walked several feet away from Chester and took a deep breath. With all her might she began to run. As she grew near her pony, she vaulted for his back. It was the hop of Cassie's life, but she didn't even come close to making it onto Chester's back. She ended up rolling on the barn floor, laughing as she rolled.

After a couple of tries, J.J. said, "I've got an idea how you can get on."

She clucked to Chester and rode him out of the barn and over toward the fence. Cassie followed. She noticed that with J.J. on Chester, he looked like a real horse, not just a chubby little spotted pony. J.J. was a natural equestrian.

Cassie climbed the fence and awkwardly joined J.J. on Chester's back. "See? Nothing to it," said J.J.

"Wait, wait," said Cassie, trying to get settled into place. She held onto J.J.'s waist and gulped down her fears. "Okay, I'm ready."

Best Friends Forever?

J.J. clucked to Chester. The pony raised his head and obediently began to walk toward Possum Creek. Cassie squealed as Chester moved ahead suddenly. Her weight shifted quickly with Chester's movement, and she felt like she was going to wobble right off his back.

"Hold onto me, Cassie," J.J. said fearlessly. "You can do it!"

By the time the pair had ridden across the pasture, Cassie was starting to feel more comfortable. "Hey, this is fun!" she exclaimed. She was glad to have a friend like J.J. who helped her overcome her secret fears.

The frogs, crickets, and katydids had already started their evening chorus long before the sun went down. As they arrived at Possum Creek, the girls slipped off Chester's back and tied him up to a small but sturdy tree trunk. Chester nosed around and found some sweet grass to munch while Cassie and J.J. hopped across the flat stones in the creek to Talking Rock. Talking Rock jutted into the wide, river-like creek.

Sitting on Talking Rock with her very best friend was Cassie's favorite thing to do. It really didn't matter whether they talked or just listened to the sounds of the water rushing past and the night song of the tiny creatures in the woods. What was important was to share the moments together.

The large, smooth, flat rock, which was much bigger than all the others in the creek, felt cool and was just right for lying or sitting on. Cassie laid her head back and watched the trees sway in the summer breeze above them. J.J. sat cross-legged, tossing tiny, yellow wildflower petals into Possum Creek and watching them drift downstream.

"I'm glad we're going to see Nurse Trixie and the children at New Hope Center Saturday," said J.J. finally.

Cassie thought for a moment. "I suppose it will be fun, especially with you and Iggy there," she replied finally.

"Cassie?" J.J. asked. "Don't you want to go?"

"Sure," said Cassie, sitting up beside J.J. "It's just that I don't know what visiting the children at New Hope Center will be like exactly. What will we say to them? I mean, they're sick. Maybe they can't play and run and jump. I hope it's not like a real hospital. Hospitals smell funny."

J.J. smiled. "It will be an adventure," she said. "Just like riding Chester bareback."

Cassie smiled back. When she was with J.J., she felt like anything was possible. It might be uncomfortable at first, but she would have fun at New Hope Center on Saturday. If J.J. was so certain they would have fun, Cassie knew everything would turn out okay.

Later that night, the girls lay in bed giggling. Whenever they spent the night together, they were never able to fall asleep until the middle of the night.

Suddenly J.J. sat up in bed. "Does my mom know I am staying over with you tonight?"

Cassie broke out into a new round of giggles. "Yes, my mother called your mom, and they worked it out while we were riding Chester."

"Oh, whew," said J.J., relieved. "Thanks for letting me borrow a set of your pajamas. It's good that we're about the same size."

J.J. laid back down. They finally got still and quiet. Just as Cassie was about to drift off to sleep, J.J. piped up with, "Cassie, what can we take to the children at New Hope Center on Saturday?"

Cassie jerked awake and yawned. "I don't know. Maybe some Snickerdoodles?"

"I'm tired of baking cookies," said J.J. "Besides, maybe some of the children there can't eat sweets. Let's take something cheerful, you know, something that is special, that might brighten up the day for them."

"Good idea," agreed Cassie. "But I don't have any money. I spent all my allowance on the fair. Whatever we take, we would have to make it ourselves with supplies we already have."

The room grew quiet again as the girls thought about what they could make for the children at New Hope Center. Cassie began to drift off into a dream.

"Paper flowers!" exclaimed J.J. Cassie was so startled she nearly fell out of bed.

"What are you talking about?" she asked.

"Paper flowers to take to New Hope Center," said J.J. "My mom taught me how to make them out of tissue paper. I could show you. There's tissue paper in all colors in my mom's studio at home. Let's make them tomorrow!"

"Okay," mumbled Cassie, snuggling into her pillow. She was excited about visiting the children, but not *that* excited!

Best Friends Forever?

4

The next morning, Cassie and J.J. fed Opie (Cassie's dog), and Chester. Then they rode their bikes to J.J.'s apartment. Heading through Misty Falls Town Square, they waved to Iggy at Potts Photography Shop. He and Mr. Potts looked busy with customers, so they continued on.

J.J.'s cat, Frisco, met the girls at the door and meowed loudly for breakfast. While J.J. opened a can of Tastee Tuna and quickly fed him, Cassie admired the many paintings and sculptures that Ms. Graystone had bought or painted herself. Her collection filled the small apartment, with every corner and niche perfectly decorated. Frisco purred with delight over his food bowl as Cassie followed J.J.

"Come on," said J.J., hurrying into her mother's art studio. "The tissue paper is in this drawer."

J.J. opened the drawer. There was tissue paper in red, sky blue, orange, pink, yellow, and lavender. "Won't these make beautiful flowers?" she asked.

In a large pot by the door were foot–long dowel sticks. J.J. grabbed a handful of them. "Good," said J.J. "We will use the dowel sticks for flower stems. Now all we need are some large, thick rubber bands."

"Rubber bands for what?" asked J.J.'s mother. The girls didn't realize she was standing in the doorway. They turned to meet her smile.

"Good morning, Mom," said J.J.

"Oh, hi Ms. Graystone," said Cassie. "Gee, I hope it's alright that we are in your art studio."

"Sure," said J.J.'s mother, taking a sip of hot coffee from her ceramic mug. "Can I help you find rubber bands? Here they are."

"Good," said J.J. "Okay, we're all set. Mom, we're going to make paper flowers for the children at New Hope Center."

"How lovely! I like to see my girls being creative," she said. Ms. Graystone always said "my girls." It made Cassie feel as though she belonged at J.J.'s house.

"Cassie," said J.J. "Get the scissors over there on the desk."

As Cassie brought over the scissors, Ms. Graystone said, "I'm so happy to hear that you are going to visit the children on Saturday. Well, if you'll excuse me, I have to get ready for work now. I heard on the radio that the traffic is backing up on the interstates leading into Atlanta. I wish I could help, but I need to leave as soon as I can if I'm going to make it to work on time.

Best Friends Forever?

There are bills to pay, and I don't want to be late!"

"Okay," sang the girls in chorus.

"Be careful with the scissors," called Ms. Graystone.

"We will," said J.J. She pulled out her mom's favorite craft book and opened it to the page with instructions for making paper flowers.

"What do we do first?" asked Cassie. "I've never made paper flowers before. Are they hard to make?"

"Not at all," said J.J. "The directions are easy to follow. See?"

Tissue Paper Flowers

You will need: colored tissue paper, dowel sticks, scissors

(You can make smaller flowers by using half sheets of tissue and chenille stems instead of dowel sticks.)

1. Count out five layers of tissue. Smooth the paper gently and make sure the layers are evenly stacked on top of each other.

2. Fold the paper in half along the length (the longer side). Cut the paper along the folded edge, creating two equal parts.

3. Stack the two equal sets of papers, making ten layers of "petals."

—*continued on next page* **29**

Tissue Paper Flowers

—continued from previous page

4. Along the width of the paper (the shorter side), make one-inch folds, flipping the paper back and forth to make an accordion-like fan.

5. Once the paper is accordion-folded and looks like one long strip, place a dowel stick in the middle of the strip. Make sure one end of the stick is placed an inch or two above the edge of the paper strip.

6. Use a rubber band to fasten the paper to the dowel stick, making a "stem" out of the stick. Loop and twist the rubber band around the stick until it holds the paper firmly to the stem.

7. Gently pull open the accordion folds on either side of the stem, leaving a circle of paper around the top edge of the stem.

8. Carefully pull the top layer of paper as high as it will go. Separate the layers of paper and gently pull them up one by one.

9. Trim off any squared edges to make the "petals" appear more rounded. Spray the flower with cologne to make it realistically fragrant!

Best Friends Forever?

J.J. carefully followed the insturctions and explained every step to Cassie. Soon the two girls were looking at a beautiful, colorful paper flower. Cassie couldn't believe how easily J.J. had finished it. J.J. had a way of making so many things seem effortless.

"Ta–da!" sang J.J., as Cassie admired their work.

"How did you do that?" Cassie asked, amazed. "We didn't even measure the paper."

"Oh, you don't have to measure it," said J.J. "If you want to make smaller flowers, just cut the paper into smaller equal pieces and use pipe cleaners for stems. If you want to make big flowers like we did, use dowel sticks. Mom bought hers at the craft store."

"It's nice of your mom to let us use her supplies," said Cassie.

Just then, Ms. Graystone appeared, all ready for work. "Very nice work, girls," she said, adoring the flower. Her eyes seemed to study every detail. "I love the fragrance too. Just like a real flower."

J.J. and Cassie hardly noticed when she left for work. They were already busy with their next flower...and the next, and the next, and the next...

The time flew by, at least until J.J.'s tummy growled. Both girls stopped what they were doing when they realized they were getting hungry. "It's past lunch time, I guess," said J.J. "Want a peanut butter sand-wich?"

"With jelly, if you have it," said Cassie.

"Grape or strawberry?" asked J.J.

"I think I feel like grape today," said Cassie.

"I'm having strawberry," said J.J.

The girls left their work and scampered to the kitchen. After gobbling the sandwiches and a big glass of milk each, they couldn't wait to get back to their "garden" of paper flowers.

"Wow," exclaimed Cassie, as she returned to the art studio. It was filled with a colorful array of "blooms." "I didn't realize we had made so many flowers."

"Me either!" said J.J. "Won't Nurse Trixie be surprised!"

Cassie had to admit it had been fun to make the flowers for the friends she hadn't met yet at New Hope Center. She hoped they would like their surprises!

Best Friends Forever?

5

Saturday finally came. When Mrs. Holbrook drove Cassie to J.J.'s, it took all three of them two trips each to load the car with the paper flowers that J.J. and Cassie had made. There was hardly anywhere left to sit! J.J. and Cassie couldn't see out the car windows because the flowers blocked their view.

When they picked up Iggy, a few flowers got smashed as Iggy tried to slide into the car underneath them. "Are we having a garden party?" he asked. Then his nose began to wiggle. "Ah, ah, ah-choo!" he sneezed.

"God bless you," said Mrs. Holbrook.

"Thank—ahhhh-ahhh-choo," said Iggy.

"God bless you again!" exclaimed Mrs. Holbrook.

"Uh-oh," said Cassie. "I forgot, Iggy is allergic to colognes and flowers."

"We'd better hurry, then," said Mrs. Holbrook. "Iggy will have sneezed his head off by the time we get to New Hope Center."

"I hope not," sniffled Iggy. "I kind of count on

having my head on my shoulders at all times.
Ah—choo!"

At last, Iggy, J.J., and Cassie arrived at New Hope
Center. Mrs. Holbrook drove them up, up, up the long
drive to the main entrance, where Nurse Trixie had
promised to meet them.

While Iggy sneezed, Cassie and J.J. peeked past pesky
flower petals to see summer wildflowers dotting the
green lawns everywhere. Cassie pointed out an empty
playground under a patch of oak trees. She wondered
why the children weren't playing on such a lovely
afternoon.

The children got out of the car. Cassie and J.J.
gathered up as many flowers as they could hold and
looked up at the large white building at the top of the
hill.

Iggy popped a fresh canister of film into the loading
chamber of his camera. "This is going to be fun," he
said.

"Yes, and it might be a little sad," said J.J. Her indigo
eyes seemed to be able to see through the building's
walls into the faces of the children inside.

Cassie swallowed, but it felt like the sides of her
throat were closing in and sticking together. She
wasn't so sure how the afternoon would turn out.
With every second that ticked by, her stomach was
growing tighter. What if she couldn't think of anything
to say to the sick boys and girls she met?

Best Friends Forever?

She always felt a little awkward around new people anyway. But once when Cassie had confessed this secret, her mom had said, "Why, Cassidy Marie Holbrook! You don't have a shy bone in your body!"

Whether her mom believed it or not, all of Cassie's bones felt pretty shy. But it was too late to turn back now. Cassie found herself getting out of her family's sport utility vehicle with dozens of paper flowers and walking up the long row of steps to the glass double doors.

At the sight of Nurse Trixie's glowing smile, Cassie's tummy relaxed just a bit. Trixie was such a cheerful person. Even the rabbits printed on the material of Nurse Trixie's jacket were smiling.

"Welcome to New Hope Center," said Nurse Trixie, as she held open the big door. "Oh, what beautiful flowers you've brought! The children will love them!"

Iggy snapped a photograph of Trixie, which made her laugh. "I'm glad to see your freckles are not green today, Iggy. Come on in!"

They stepped into the peach-colored main room. Instantly it felt like a real home. Large vases of freshly cut flowers were on every table. Cozy garden-green sofas with overstuffed cushions invited them to sit down. In the center of the room was an aquarium the size of a bathtub, filled with brightly colored tropical fish. Still holding armloads of flowers, J.J. and Cassie helped Trixie fill some extra vases full. They placed the vases around the aquarium. The fish seemed to be attracted to the bright colors outside their underwater home.

Cassie's mother and Nurse Trixie were instant friends, just as Cassie had expected. When Nurse Trixie told her "what a beautiful job" Iggy, J.J., and Cassie had done at the recent blood drive, Mrs. Holbrook beamed proudly.

"And did you make these flowers yourselves?" marveled Trixie. "My, what delightful, talented young people!"

"Oh yes, I agree," said Mrs. Holbrook.

Cassie and J.J. rolled their eyes at each other as if to say, "It's just like grown-ups to talk that way."

But Iggy spoke his mind out loud. "Okay, okay. You don't have to say all that stuff, Nurse Trixie. Mrs. Holbrook already knows how remarkable we are."

"Do I ever!" exclaimed Mrs. Holbrook, tousling Iggy's wild red curls.

Cassie and J.J. laughed. Iggy had a way of making life's moments, well… funnier.

Mrs. Holbrook glanced at her watch. "Oh goodness, I'm late for my Sunday School teachers meeting at the church. What time should I pick up these three remarkable human beings, Nurse Trixie?"

"Give us a couple of hours at least," said Trixie. "They will be busy!"

Iggy, J.J., and Cassie waved good-bye to Mrs.

Best Friends Forever?

Holbrook and willingly followed Trixie from one room to the next. Halfway through the tour of New Hope Center, Cassie had forgotten all about her queasy stomach. But she wondered, *where are all the children?*

Besides the main room, there were other rooms that made New Hope Center seem just like home, too. Iggy liked the large eat-in kitchen, especially since the cook was baking brownies. Cassie's favorite was the brightly wallpapered playroom with craft tables. Every game and toy imaginable lined the shelves. A huge painting in bold colors hung on the wall, picturing Jesus with children gathered around Him.

Heading down a long hallway, J.J. peered out the window. "Oh look at the flower garden!" she said. "And a petting zoo!"

Iggy and Cassie joined her at the window. Sure enough, a pathway led through a maze of flowers and plants of many varieties and colors. The garden was laced with latticework, birdbaths, feeders, and decorative stones. Beyond the garden were sheds and fenced areas that housed rabbits, chickens, ducks, and small deer.

"Hey, I thought this place was going to look like a hospital," blurted Iggy.

Trixie smiled. "We designed New Hope Center to try and make the kids feel like they are at the next best place to being home."

"This is better than home," said Iggy. "A guy could get used to living here."

"Yeah," agreed the girls.

Trixie nodded. "By the time the children come to us, they have been in a hospital for days, sometimes weeks or months. We want our young patients to think of the New Hope Center as a vacation home…a vacation home where all the children help with the chores!"

"Chores? On vacation? Ugh!" exclaimed Iggy.

Trixie laughed. "They have play times, too. But we feel it's important for each child to have a responsibility. It helps them think about something besides their medical condition and missing their families. Some of the children help with the gardening. Others take care of the animals. Some feed the fish in the big aquarium indoors. We even have a few boys and girls who like to help our cook!"

"But what if someone needs a doctor?" asked J.J.

"We have doctors who visit each week," said Trixie. She opened a cabinet. "And see? Hidden away are all the medical supplies and equipment that the children need to help them get well."

"It must cost a lot to live here," said Cassie. The building and furnishings were a lot nicer and newer than her family's home.

Trixie shook her head. "Actually, people and businesses in the community give money to New Hope

Best Friends Forever?

Center, so families don't have to pay so much."

Iggy, Cassie, and J.J. looked around. Yes, the center seemed to have everything, except...

"Where are the children?" asked Iggy.

Trixie waved them further down the hall. She whispered, "It's rest time, but there's one patient who I'm sure is not napping. She is one of our patients that I want you to be sure to meet. Come this way."

Uh-oh. Cassie held her stomach. She could feel it growing tighter and queasier again, but she was also very curious about the children who lived here...

★★★★★★★★★★★★★★★★

A door with a handmade sign read, "Robyn's Room." Flowers, stars, and streamers in bright colors decorated the sign. Nurse Trixie knocked on the door.

"Come in," piped a sweet, soft voice. J.J., Cassie, and Iggy followed Trixie into the bright, yellow room with an orange, lavender, and lime candy wallpaper border.

A tiny girl with a head full of shoulder-length blond hair busily typed on a computer at her desk. Her pixie-like fingers flew across the computer keys with great precision.

Cassie knew right away that Robyn was one smart girl. How could she type so well at such a young age? She looked like she was only about eight years old.

Just then, the girl looked up and grinned widely. "Oh! I have real live company!" she chirped. She turned away from the computer, swinging herself around on the big chair that seemed to swallow her whole.

"I'm Robyn with a 'y'. Robyn Alexa Morgan. I thought it was just the nurse with my medicine. I didn't know it was already time to meet my brand-new friends! Trixie told me you were coming," she remarked cheerfully.

Trixie pretended to frown as she looked at her watch. "You were supposed to be resting until they came, young lady!"

"Oh Trixie, you know how tired I am of resting," Robyn said, making a funny face. "I've been lying around for months, and I'm ready for action!"

"I see," said Nurse Trixie. "Robyn, I'd like you to meet Iggy Potts, J.J. Graystone, and Cassie Holbrook. I met them the other day at the blood drive."

"Hi!" said Robyn. Her blue eyes were the color of a robin's eggs, which made her name perfect for her, Cassie thought. Those eyes lit up with delight as she spied what Cassie was holding.

"For me?! Thank you!" Robyn exclaimed.

Cassie had forgotten that she was still holding one of the paper flowers. Robyn accepted the large pink flower and sniffed its rosy scent. "Oh, just like a real rose."

Robyn smiled brightly as she looked right into Cassie's eyes. Cassie shyly found herself staring at her own dirty sneakers. But J.J. met Robyn's smile with a wide, toothy grin.

Robyn touched the deep red feathers in J.J.'s hair clasp. "These are beautiful. Are they real?"

"Yes, but they're dyed that crimson color," said J.J. "It was a gift from my grandmother. She lives in Arizona on a Navajo reservation. My grandmother made it to sell at Canyon de Chelley, near Flagstaff. She gave it to me for my birthday when I was just a little girl. I've been saving it for a special occasion."

"It's very pretty against your silky, dark hair, J.J.," Robyn said, crossing her legs in the big chair. "Do you miss your grandmother?"

"Yes, very much," said J.J. "My grandmother took care of me when I was little. My dad still lives in Arizona too. I really don't remember much about him. I haven't seen him since I was a little girl. My parents are divorced now."

"So you live with your mom?" asked Robyn.

"Yes, here in Misty Falls. It's a wonderful place to live," said J.J.

Robyn's eyes softened, but her voice was steady. "I don't live with either of my parents. They've been in heaven for a long time. We were in a car accident when I was three years old."

A sharp breath caught in Cassie's throat. Iggy's face reflected his surprise as well. No one knew what to say, so J.J. reached for Robyn's hand. She patted the tiny, white hand in her own bronze one.

When Robyn saw the children's downhearted expressions, she quickly added, "Don't be sad! I don't really remember much about my mom and dad. Sometimes I do daydream about being with them again one day. We're all going to live in heaven together. That's what Aunt Felicia says, anyway."

"I'm sorry, Robyn," said J.J., blinking widely. "I kind of know how it is living without a dad. When I get lonely for a dad, I go over to Cassie's."

Cassie's heart felt broken and amazed for Robyn, and J.J., too. Cassie couldn't even imagine being without her father. He was the most important adult in her life.

Then Cassie realized something. J.J. had never talked about her parents' divorce before! Not even on Talking Rock. Just now, it had seemed easy for J.J. to share her thoughts with Robyn. Almost too easy.

For a moment, Cassie wished that J.J. had chosen to share those feelings with her alone, not Robyn. She tried to shake it out of her mind. As Cassie pondered this, she almost didn't hear what else Robyn was saying.

"My aunt and uncle are my parents now. They're great! It's fun to be with them because I get to help my aunt in her home business. She boards and grooms pets. That's what I'm doing now, designing a web site for Aunt Felicia's Pet Cottage."

Best Friends Forever?

"Awesome," said Iggy. He studied the computer screen with great interest. "Wow, you have designed it so that people can set up an appointment for their pet on the web page. Hey, how do you know how to do this, Robyn? You're not old enough!"

"I am too old enough—and smart enough, too! I'm ten and a quarter years old, I'll have you know," Robyn said, her nose turned up. "Anyway, I have had lots of surgeries, and the computer is something I can play around on while I am waiting to get well."

Trixie walked toward the door. "And that won't be very long, young lady. You have had your final surgery, and you'll be out of here in no time!"

"I can't wait!" said Robyn. "Last year, I was tutored in bed. This year, I get to start classes at Misty Falls Elementary School. I'll be in the fifth grade."

"That's fantastic! Misty Falls Elementary is next door to our school!" exclaimed J.J. "We are going into the seventh grade at Misty Falls Middle School. But we'll see each other, you know, since our schools are so close together."

"Yeah," agreed Iggy. "I'm sure we'll see you on the playground, Robyn. And sometimes our schools have special programs together at the football field. You'll like fifth grade. I hope you get Miss Russell; she's my favorite teacher of all time. She even plays the guitar and sings during English class!"

"I like her already!" chirped Robyn.

Adventures in Misty Falls

"Okay," said Trixie, "you kids are acting like old friends, so I'm going to make myself scarce for a while. See you later at the nurse's station."

Robyn placed her flower beside the computer. Then she reached for her crutches next to the desk, and she was off. "Come on," she said, "There's lots to see."

The tiny girl wasted no time showing the others around the grounds of New Hope Center. If Robyn was tired and needed a nap like the other patients, she certainly didn't show it! Cassie could hardly keep up with her sometimes. The only signs that Robyn had been in an accident were the crutches, of course, and some scars on her legs, arms, and neck from surgeries.

In the garden, Robyn showed them all her secret hiding places, even where she used to play school under the giant bushes outside with her dolls. There was still a little tea set nesting in a bushy clump of grass.

"That's Madison's tea set," explained Robyn. "She's three years old and is deaf. There aren't any other little girls her age for her to play with. So I showed her my favorite hiding place, and we play tea party almost every day. Come on! I'll race you to the swings!"

Iggy, J.J., Cassie, and Robyn ended up on the swings for almost an hour. Iggy pushed Cassie in the swing, and then Cassie pushed Iggy.

Meanwhile, J.J. pushed Robyn, as Robyn begged, "Higher, J.J. Push me higher!"

44

"I think you're going high enough," said J.J. "Besides, my arms are getting tired from pushing you."

Cassie wiped her forehead. "It's getting hot out here," she said. "Maybe we should go back inside."

Reluctantly, Robyn got out of the swing. She stiffly straightened up as Iggy got her crutches ready. Then the four returned to Robyn's air-conditioned room and played Pass the Pigs.

Although Cassie tried to pretend to have fun, she couldn't help noticing how friendly J.J. was getting with Robyn. For the past hour, J.J. had seemed to forget that Cassie was even there! Even Iggy seemed different around this strange but nice new girl. Cassie felt a little guilty for feeling so troubled. She just couldn't understand all the mixed-up feelings she was having.

The foursome were in the midst of their third game of Pass the Pigs when Nurse Trixie's voice came over the intercom speaker. "Okay, ladies and gentlemen, your ride is here. Mrs. Holbrook is waiting in the lobby," she said.

Relieved, Cassie hopped up off the floor and dusted off her shorts. She was glad to be going home.

"Have two hours gone by already?" asked J.J. as she helped Robyn put away the game. "This was fun!"

"Here," said Robyn, reaching for her crutches, "I'll walk you down the hall."

"Wait a minute! Hold that smile," said Iggy.

The camera flash startled Robyn and she started to giggle. She then led the others out of the room toward the main room.

"Is that really your camera?" she asked along the way.

"Yes, well, sort of," said Iggy. "My dad owns a photography shop. I help him, and he lets me use this camera. When I earn enough money, I'm going to buy it for my very own."

Robyn lightly took tiny hops on her crutches as she continued to chatter.

"I have an idea! I have a scanner on my computer. If you will bring some of your favorite photos, we can scan them and make posters, cards, stationery, or whatever you want."

"Alright!" exclaimed Iggy, as they reached the lobby. Instantly, Robyn spotted the vases of paper flowers that J.J. and Cassie had made.

"Ooooh!" she exclaimed and moved toward them as quickly as she could on her crutches. "Nurse Trixie, when can the other children get up from their naps and see the flowers?"

But Trixie didn't hear Robyn. She and Mrs. Holbrook were chatting as they sat on the sofa. They were wrapped up in a conversation all their own. Robyn boldly made her way toward them. She didn't seem to be shy around adults or anyone, Cassie noted.

Trixie introduced Robyn to Cassie's mom.

"Why hello, Robyn. I'm so glad to meet you," said

Mrs. Holbrook warmly. "What lovely blond hair you have!"

"Thank you, I like it too," said Robyn. "Thank you for bringing my new friends to see me—and all the pretty paper flowers. When can J.J., Cassie, and Iggy come back?"

"I'm glad you asked that," said Trixie. "Mrs. Holbrook has agreed to bring them back for our New Hope Summer Picnic tomorrow afternoon after church. Is that soon enough for you?"

Robyn and J.J. gasped and looked at each other excitedly.

Then J.J. grabbed Cassie's arm. "Oh Cassie, won't that be great?"

"Hey, Robyn," said Iggy, "you forgot to show us the petting zoo today. Can we pet the animals at the picnic tomorrow, Trixie?" Iggy asked, hopefully.

"Yes, and you can feed them, too. Besides the petting zoo, there will be outdoor games and a picnic lunch, with watermelon slices and homemade ice cream. So bring your appetites!"

"Don't worry, I will," said Iggy. "Eating is my favorite pastime—besides taking pictures, that is!"

Everyone laughed.

"Oh Robyn, I almost forgot," said J.J. "Do you have email? I want to send you a message tonight."

Robyn pulled some scrap paper out of her pocket and quickly wrote her email address.

She handed the paper to J.J.

"Please write me!" she said, hugging J.J. good-bye. "Cassie, it was really great to meet you. I'll see you Sunday, I mean, tomorrow!"

"Here Iggy," said Nurse Trixie, reaching for the camera. "Let me take your picture with Robyn, J.J., and Cassie. Is this the button I press?"

Iggy showed her how to operate the camera. They all huddled together, and Iggy yelled out, "Hey, everybody, let's say 'cheese dip'!"

"Cheese dip!" everyone sang—everyone except Cassie. The best she could do was force a weak smile.

Best Friends Forever?

6

As soon as they had piled into the car, J.J. became a regular chatterbox.

"I just love Robyn, don't you? Isn't she cute? She has such a great imagination. And she's so smart, too!" said J.J. enthusiastically.

"Oh yes, Robyn is darling, just darling," said Mrs. Holbrook as she drove past the entrance gate.

Great, Cassie thought. Now even Mother was acting the same way that J.J. and Iggy were behaving. Cassie felt a little like crying. But she couldn't put her finger on what was making her feel so bad.

Was it because Robyn's life had been threatened by a car accident? And that her parents had been killed? Did she feel like crying because Robyn's cheerful attitude made her feel guilty? Or was it because Cassie's best friends spent most of the afternoon talking and laughing with a complete stranger and ignoring her?

Cassie wondered, *maybe it was all of those things.* At any rate, she felt miserable.

Adventures in Misty Falls

Mrs. Holbrook glanced at Cassie in the rearview mirror. "You are awfully quiet, Cassie," she said. Did you enjoy your visit at New Hope Center?"

Cassie managed a smile and a short reply. "Yes, it's a nice place, alright."

In a bubbly way, J.J. added, "Nice? It's great! Robyn is great! I can't wait to meet the other children! And we get to return tomorrow for a picnic! I'm so excited!"

Then Mrs. Holbrook made a suggestion. "We'll go to New Hope Center right after church. J.J., you might as well stay over at our house tonight. Do you want to ask your mom about it? That way, you can go to church with Cassie. We will meet Iggy there and head on over to the picnic at New Hope Center."

"That sounds good," said J.J. "I'm sure Mom won't mind. I think she's got a date tonight, so I would be by myself with Frisco and our neighbor from next door, anyway."

"Good," said Mrs. Holbrook. "I'm glad it will work out for you to stay with us."

"Boy, am I hungry," said Iggy. At that moment his stomach growled so loudly that Mrs. Holbrook began to laugh.

"This is definitely an emergency," said Mrs. Holbrook. "Let's stop at Pepper's Grill. It's just ahead."

"Alright!" said Iggy. "Mrs. Holbrook, for a mom, you're really cool."

Best Friends Forever?

"Thank you, Mr. Potts," said Mrs. Holbrook. "I try."

Usually Cassie could eat a whole platter of Pepper's famous cheese fries by herself. But today, she could only manage a few bites. Meanwhile J.J., Iggy, and Mrs. Holbrook chattered a hundred miles a minute.

"Oh, I'm so glad you all are interested in New Hope Center. This is going to be so exciting for Robyn and the others, too. Just think of it," said Mrs. Holbrook. "Nurse Trixie says Robyn will be able to go home within a couple of weeks. Isn't that wonderful?"

"That's a relief," said J.J. "I couldn't bear to think of Robyn being stuck there without her aunt and uncle nearby."

"Yes," said Mrs. Holbrook, "Trixie said her aunt and uncle spend most of their time working to earn the money to help pay for Robyn's back and leg surgeries. They love her very much."

J.J. thought a moment and said, "Hey, I know what we can do! Let's plan to keep Robyn busy between now and the time she goes home from New Hope Center. We could get a ride over there every other day or so."

"If we have time." Cassie's voice was gloomy.

Mrs. Holbrook sipped her iced tea, then set it on the table. "Why, Cassie, you have time—time for friends. My goodness, New Hope Center isn't that far out of my way. I could drop you off nearly any day you want to go."

Adventures in Misty Falls

"Great," said Cassie blandly. Inside she was thinking, *Why should I go? Robyn is J.J.'s new best friend, not mine.*

Best Friends Forever?

7

Mrs. Holbrook dropped off Iggy at Potts' Photography Studio and drove by J.J.'s apartment building. She pulled up to the curb and parked.

"I'll be right back," said J.J. "It won't take long for me to get permission to spend the night and pack my overnight bag. Want to come in, Cassie?"

"I'll just wait in the car," mumbled Cassie.

"Take your time, dear," said Mrs. Holbrook pleasantly.

Normally, Cassie would have loved the fact that J.J. was spending the night with her. But tonight she sort of wanted to be alone. She knew she had to keep her feelings secret.

As soon as J.J. had run inside, Cassie's mom turned around to get a good look at her daughter. Cassie was slumped down in the back seat.

"What's the matter with you? Who licked all the red off your candy cane?"

"What does that mean?" Cassie asked. "I don't even have a candy cane."

Sometimes her mom's little sayings didn't make any sense.

"You are moping around like a sad sack," said her mother.

"I didn't know sacks could be sad," said Cassie.

"Never mind," said Mrs. Holbrook. "What I'm trying to say is, 'what's wrong with you, Cassidy Marie Holbrook?'"

When Mother used Cassie's full name, she meant business. "Nothing's wrong, Mom, really." Cassie sat up straight and tried to brighten. "What is a sad sack anyway?"

"Cassie Marie! Don't change the subject!" her mom snapped unexpectedly. It was obvious that she wasn't in the mood for word games.

"I'm fine, just tired, that's all," Cassie said meekly.

"Hmm," said Mom, doubtfully.

Before she could pursue her questions further, J.J. burst out of the front door of the small apartment. As they were driving away, Frisco the cat stretched his yellow and white coat out on the windowsill to stare at them.

"I'm all ready for church and the picnic tomorrow," said J.J. "Mom says it's fine, and thanks for having me. Mrs. Holbrook, will it be okay if I wear pants to church in the morning? I don't have a clean skirt."

Mrs. Holbrook smiled. "Of course, you can wear pants. Jesus doesn't care about what we wear to His house. He just cares that we are there to enjoy worshipping Him."

"I like going to your church. I know my mom and I go every now and then, but we don't really have a church where we belong," J.J. said. "Oh, Cassie, while I was inside, I emailed Robyn. I told her we couldn't wait to see her at the picnic!"

Cassie slid down in the seat and looked out the window. This was going to be a long night, and tomorrow was going to be an even longer day.

As soon as they had pulled into the driveway of the Holbrook farm, Opie began to bark at the back door. Cassie's dad always said that being a Jack Russell terrier was hard work, but if somebody had to do it, Opie was a natural. He was the household's official greeter. At eighteen pounds, Opie looked just like a little Holstein cow with his black spots and white coat.

Of course, Opie had no enemies, except the three barn cats who had learned to outsmart him. His favorite visitor was J.J.—she could barely make it into the house with her overnight bag. Opie was making such a fuss over her that she ended up sitting on the floor getting a dog-tongue bath.

"Okay, okay," laughed J.J., sputtering and spewing when Opie kissed her on the mouth. "That's enough! I know I'm welcome. You can stop now, Opie."

"Opie!" said Mrs. Holbrook in her most commanding voice. "Go to bed."

Opie ran halfway to his little bed in the kitchen and turned as if to ask, "Are you sure?"

"Go to bed," repeated Mrs. Holbrook. "You are being too frisky."

Opie's toenails clickety-clacked across the kitchen floor. He curled up obediently on his little blue bed, but his black, pointy ears stayed in a perked position, and his tail wagged as he followed the girls around the room with his wide, doggy eyes.

"I love that dog," said J.J., giggling as she wiped dog slobber off her face. "He's so cute!"

"I know," said Cassie. "He and Chester are my best friends, besides you, J.J."

After J.J. put her things in Cassie's room, the girls went to feed Cassie's pony. As they reached the barn, J.J. said, "You don't know how great it is to have Chester right here in the barn next to your house. My Gracie has to be boarded since we live in that cramped apartment."

"But you still get to see her every day, don't you?" asked Cassie, scooping out Chester's nightly portion of grain.

"Oh yes," said J.J. "I can walk down the road to see her anytime I want. But my mom says it is awfully expensive to keep a purebred quarter horse like Gracie, especially since we have to board her. I think she is trying to break some bad news to me. I think we're going to have to sell Gracie."

Best Friends Forever?

Cassie was horrified. "Don't even think that!" she said. "There must be a way."

Whenever Cassie had to think, she always climbed into the hayloft. With her Chester-chores done, into the hayloft she climbed. J.J. followed her up the ladder in silence.

Settling into the hay, J.J. shrugged her shoulders and sighed. "I've already tried to find a job, but I'm too young," she said. "Mr. Phelps will hire me at the grocery store when I'm fourteen, but that's still two years away."

Chester stuck his nose over the side of the stall and peered up at the girls, his ears perked, as if he could understand.

Suddenly, Cassie knew the answer. It was practically staring her in the face.

"Chester needs a buddy," said Cassie, "and you know how he loves Gracie!"

Both girls burst into laughter. They tried to imagine what an odd couple Chester and Gracie would make! Chester was short, stocky, and lazy, with a typical pony's potbelly. And Gracie was just like her name—graceful, slender, and sleek—with long legs, a flowing mane and tail, and lots of energy.

Then J.J. looked doubtful. "Do you think it is really possible for Gracie to stay here?"

Cassie wasn't going to take "no" for an answer. "Look, there's an extra stall and plenty of pastureland for Gracie, too. Then you could come over anytime you want, and we can go for rides!" she said excitedly.

J.J. was so excited at the prospect that she nearly lost her balance and fell off the edge of the hayloft. "Do you really mean it? I can't pay much."

"Sure," said Cassie. "Other people have boarded animals here when they went out of town or needed a place to permanently board their pet. I'll talk to Dad about it as soon as the time is right."

J.J. had never looked more radiant. Her bronze skin seemed to have a glowing sheen to it in the moonlight. The hint of a dreamy smile curled in the corners of her lips.

"I would feel better knowing Gracie is here with you, right outside your bedroom window," she said.

"Oh yes," said Cassie, diving into the hay and propping her chin in her hands. "Sometimes when I'm lying in bed at night with the windows open, I can hear Chester nicker to the cats or kick the side of the stall. Then I know everything's fine."

J.J. swiveled around and let her legs swing over the side of the loft.

She leaned her head to one side and said with a sigh, "When I was really small in Arizona, my mother tells me we had many horses on our ranch. I don't remember much about where we lived, except Grandmother's hogan and her yummy pan bread and honey."

Best Friends Forever?

"Mmm," said Cassie. "Do you miss your grand-mother?"

"I sure do. I hope to travel to Flagstaff someday to see her. I hope to see my father, too, but I'm kind of scared."

"You? Scared?" Cassie asked, surprised.

"Well, I don't know him at all. And I don't know whether he wants to see me. He has never come to visit me."

"Why not?" Cassie asked. "How can a father not want to see his own daughter?"

"He isn't like your father, Cassie. Mom says my dad is an unhappy person," said J.J. sadly. "My father acts like a boy who never grew up. He has made some bad choices. When my parents split up, he stayed in Arizona to drive trucks all over the western United States. I haven't seen him since I was five years old."

Cassie struggled to find some hope. "Doesn't he want to come and visit you?"

"I don't know. I guess not," said J.J. "Anyway, we wouldn't have anything to talk about. I'm happy with my mom, but I do miss my grandmother. I wish I could have a father who loved me, but I really don't miss my dad because I don't even know who he is, really. I doubt I'd even recognize him if I saw him."

"Would you remember your grandmother?" asked Cassie.

"Oh yes," said J.J., cheerfully. "She's the dearest

grandmother in the world. I will always remember sitting in her lap by the fireplace. I will remember her fry bread and honey. And I remember her hands, weathered by the sun and wind."

There, nestled in the hayloft with the barn cats, Cassie and J.J. talked as they always did, never running out of things to say to each other. Cassie had forgotten all about her own concern—J.J.'s new friendship with Robyn.

Now all Cassie wanted was for J.J. to have a kind father like her own dad. She wanted J.J. to be able to visit her grandmother in Arizona again. Tonight, Cassie felt needed. She was glad to know that she and J.J. were still best friends.

"I'm glad you came to spend the night," said Cassie.

Best Friends Forever?

8

Streams of sunlight brought Cassie out of her foggy dreams. Birds sang a multitude of songs in the crisp morning air. With her eyes still closed, she stretched with all her might and yawned a mighty yawn. Her right hand brushed against sharp prickles. What was it that had invaded her nice, soft bed?

Squinting her sleepy eyes, Cassie realized that she and J.J. had fallen asleep in the hayloft last night! In fact, J.J. still slumbered with pieces of hay sticking in her hair, now covered with dust. A blanket covered the girls, brought to them by a thoughtful parent in the night.

For a few moments, Cassie lay there, thinking about the girls' conversation last evening. How sad for J.J. that her father neglected her. Cassie was thankful that her own mom and dad both cared very much for all of their children. She tried for a moment to imagine what it would feel like for her father not to be around her family anymore, but it was too impossible to imagine. Dad was the best, most loyal daddy in the universe.

Knowing J.J.'s situation made Cassie feel a little guilty too. Sometimes she forgot to appreciate her parents the way she knew she should. So right then and there, Cassie prayed and thanked God for her parents. She didn't know quite how to pray for J.J.'s family, but she tried to until a familiar deep voice filled the barn.

"Are you two still snoozing?"

Cassie bolted upright to see her dad in overalls and a short-sleeved shirt ambling into the barn, his cup of morning coffee in hand.

"It's past time to get ready for church, so get a move on. Your mom says to take your extra clothes for the picnic afterwards. I'll feed Chester for you, Munchkin," said her father.

"Thanks, Dad," said Cassie, smiling sleepily. "You're not ready for church, either."

"I know," said Mr. Holbrook. "Guess we all had better shake a leg."

J.J. yawned and sat up, looking around. "Don't you ever clean your room, Cassie? It looks like a barn."

"It is the barn, silly," said Cassie. "We fell asleep in here last night!"

J.J. looked around and yawned again. "Oh," she said, pulling hay out of her shirt. "Well, it sure was fun!'"

The girls took fast showers and dressed in a hurry. Dad beeped the horn as they grabbed their Bibles and

Best Friends Forever?

a handful of apple and orange slices. Opie barked at them as they slammed the back door and ran out to the truck.

"Your mom is already at the church. She went in early this morning to get her room ready for Sunday School," said Mr. Holbrook. "If we hit the traffic lights just right, we won't be late."

The girls walked into Misty Falls Community Church just as the bell rang for Sunday School.

In the room for ages eight to twelve, everyone stood and sang, "Jesus is the Rock, and He rolls my blues away. Bop, shoo-bop, shoo-bop, whoo!" Cassie and J.J. chimed in with the rest of the group. Afterward, Cassie's mother asked the children for their prayer requests and answers to prayer.

"My cat had a litter of kittens," said Eddie Bertram as he scratched a mosquito bite on his arm.

"Kittens are quite a blessing," said Mrs. Holbrook.

"That's not what my mother said," Eddie replied. "She said they're too much trouble. I have to find homes for seven kittens. Please pray that I find homes for all of them. Anybody want a kitten?"

"I'm allergic to kittens, puppies, dust, and peanut butter," said Penny Allman. "My mother won't even let me have a goldfish."

"Okay," said Mrs. Holbrook. She began a list of prayer requests on the board.

Number one on the list was "Homes for Eddie's

Kittens." Number two was "Penny's Allergies."

Hands shot up all over the room. Mrs. Holbrook pointed to one. "Amanda, did you have a prayer request?" she asked.

"Yeah, my little brother Tommy is home sick with the chicken pox," said Amanda. "I already had chicken pox when I was in kindy-garden."

Pretty soon, Mrs. Holbrook had quite a hefty list of prayer requests, from Tommy's chicken pox to home-less kittens to travel safety for Sally's aunt and uncle who were on vacation.

"Anything else for our prayer request list before we take these requests to God in prayer?" asked Mrs. Holbrook.

Silence fell across the room. Then a hand went up. It was J.J.'s.

"Yes, J.J.," said Mrs. Holbrook.

J.J. cleared her throat. "I'd like everyone to pray for a very special person that Cassie, Iggy, and I met yesterday at New Hope Center. Her name is Robyn Morgan. She's had lots of surgeries after a car accident that killed her parents. She is the most cheerful person I've ever met. Robyn is full of joy even though she has been through so much sadness and pain. Pray that Cassie and I can be good friends to her."

"Very good. Thank you, J.J.," said Mrs. Holbrook. She added Robyn to the prayer request list.

Cassie's heart skipped a beat. She was touched by

Best Friends Forever?

J.J.'s concern for Robyn. Instead of asking for prayer about her own problems, J.J. was thinking of someone else.

Then Cassie began to think about something else. *Maybe, just maybe, after the picnic today, Cassie would not be J.J.'s dearest friend in the world. Perhaps Robyn would take Cassie's place in J.J.'s life!* Somehow, Cassie would just *have* to keep that from happening.

As the boys and girls prayed for the many prayer requests, Cassie's mind was on one thing only. Cassie's private prayer request list was very short. Her list only had one item on it...to keep J.J. and Robyn separated at the picnic. Even as she prayed, she felt ashamed of herself, but what choice did she have? She couldn't risk losing J.J.'s friendship because of that girl!

Best Friends Forever?

9

Cassie's mind drifted away from the Sunday School lesson even though it was about her favorite miracle that Jesus performed in the Bible. She leaned over and whispered to J.J.

"Later, let's explore the woods behind New Hope Center," said Cassie. "You know, hang out—just you and me."

J.J. looked puzzled. "What about all the other kids? What about Robyn?" she whispered back. "I'm going to stay at the picnic with everyone else."

Cassie felt her face flush. "Oh, I just meant after we eat. We can see everyone at the picnic, and then get away from the crowd. I just want to be with my best friend." She squeezed J.J.'s arm for emphasis.

J.J. didn't seem to notice. "We'd better listen," said J.J. Her indigo eyes were focused on Mrs. Holbrook. Cassie sighed and turned her attention back to the lesson.

Little had Cassie known, until then, that her mom was staring right at her. She didn't look at all pleased. She was giving Cassie that "stern mother" sort of look. Sometimes Cassie loved having her mom teach her Sunday School class. Now was definitely not one of those times.

"All right," said Mrs. Holbrook, "Who wants to act out the scene from our Bible story? I'll need someone to play the part of Jesus."

Paul raised his hand and yelled, "I will! I will!"

"Very good, Paul," said Mrs. Holbrook, "you may play the part of Jesus. I need actors to play the parts of the little boy who will share his loaves of bread and fish, and two disciples, Philip and Andrew."

"Hey, that's not fair!" said Hannah Sue, standing up and placing her hands on her hips. Hannah Sue Hanson was the biggest girl in the class. "There aren't any girls' roles in this skit. What about women's rights?"

"Women's rights? You're not a woman. Stop whining," said Paul in a very non-Jesus-like tone.

Hannah Sue frowned.

"You can't tell me what to do. You're not really Jesus, ya know. Mrs. Holbrook, can girls be in this skit or not?" she exlcaimed.

Cassie got the distinct feeling that if her mom said no, Hannah Sue would rise up right then and there and march home, or maybe she would stomp on Mrs.

Best Friends Forever?

Holbrook's foot, grab the Bible out of her hands, and take over as director.

"Of course," said Mrs. Holbrook gently. "I had hoped some of the girls would volunteer to be disciples. Hannah Sue, would you and Betsie play the parts of Andrew and Philip?"

Hannah Sue sniffed with satisfaction and sat down. She winked at Betsie who was blushing a hundred shades of red.

"Thank you, girls," said Mrs. Holbrook, matter-of-factly. "And Alex, why don't you play the boy who shares his lunch."

"Now wait a minute," said Paul. "I don't think Hannah Sue and Betsie or any other girls should play the parts of my Possels."

"Your what?" asked Mrs. Holbrook.

"My Possels."

"Oh," said Mrs. Holbrook, "you mean Jesus' apostles."

"That's what I said," said Paul. Now that he was chosen to play Jesus, he acted like his opinion was just a little too important.

"Thank you, Paul," said Mrs. Holbrook. "But I believe that Hannah Sue and Betsie will make fine apostles for our skit."

Paul looked stunned, and then he shot Hannah Sue a mean look.

Hannah Sue stuck her nose into the air with a satisfied grin on her face. Betsie looked so embarrassed

that she might have hidden under the carpet if she
could have crawled underneath it.

Whew, that was close, Cassie thought to herself. She
was starting to feel sorry for her mother who was
doing her best to keep the peace.

Mrs. Holbrook took Paul and Alex aside and gave
them special instructions. She gave Alex a covered
basket with some food inside. Next, she gave empty
baskets to the apostles.

"Now, everyone, you are the multitude, or the
crowd, that has come to hear Jesus speak. You're
excited about how He heals the sick and teaches the
Bible. You want to meet this great man, and you
wonder if He really is God's own Son. But you've
been listening for a long time, and you're very
hungry."

"How did you know?" said Logan, holding his stomach. "I slept late and didn't have time for breakfast."

"You didn't have time to comb your hair, either,"
said a rather disgusted Hannah Sue.

Cassie and J.J. looked at each other as if they were
thinking the very same thing...Hannah Sue Hanson
was just plain mean.

"The people who had come to hear Jesus weren't
concerned about their hair," said Mrs. Holbrook,
trying to hide her amusement. "Can we get back to
our play? I need the crowd of five thousand to stand
over here."

Best Friends Forever?

"Us? Five thousand?" bellowed Iggy. "You mean like five thousand people?"

"Actually, the Bible says there were five thousand men. It doesn't count the number of women and children who were also in the crowd," said Mrs. Holbrook.

"Why didn't the Bible tell how many women there were?" asked Hannah Sue.

Mrs. Holbrook pretended not to hear. "Now let's focus on our story, shall we? Use your imagination, Iggy. Just pretend to be one person standing in the middle of a huge crowd of people who are pushing in to hear Jesus."

"Cool," he said. "I bet it looked like the blood drive crowd that was here a few days ago."

"Actually, it was much, much larger than the blood drive crowd," said Mrs. Holbrook. "More like a championship football game crowd."

"Wow," said Iggy. "I wish I could have taken a picture of that crowd with Jesus. If only I lived back then. I'd be named Photojournalist of the Century!"

Mrs. Holbrook shook her head and remained focused on her work. She said, "I need the main characters up here with me. Everyone, please take your places in the crowd scene. I will narrate."

To Cassie's total surprise, the skit came off without a hitch. It went something like this:

Narrator: John 6:1–13 is the story of a little boy who gave his small snack to Jesus. He watched Jesus use it in a mighty way.

Our story begins as "Jesus looked up and saw a great crowd coming toward him." He turned to Philip and said... (John 6:5)

Jesus: These men and women and boys and girls need food. They haven't eaten for a very long time. Where shall we buy bread for them to eat?

Philip: We would have to work for eight months to earn enough to feed each of them one little bite. What are we going to do?

Narrator: Jesus' disciple, Andrew, walked up with a little boy.

Andrew: Here's a little fellow with five small barley loaves and two small fish. But how far will they go in feeding a big crowd like this? It's like the Super Bowl out here!

A twitter of laughter waved through the "crowd," because of Hannah Sue's ad-lib about the Super Bowl.

Jesus (raising His hand): Have the people sit down. (The crowd sits down. He begins to bless the food.)

Best Friends Forever?

Narrator: Jesus took out a small loaf of bread from the little boy's basket. He blessed the food and gave the disciples the boy's snack for them to distribute. Then the miracle occurred. To everyone's surprise and joy, each person there had more than they could eat.

At this point in the skit, all the children were amazed—even Cassie. She didn't know that her mom had baked bread for her Sunday School class. Jesus helped Andrew and Philip pass out the bread, and it seemed to multiply as Cassie's mom brought out more. The children had more than they could eat, even Logan, whose tummy had been growling throughout the skit.

Jesus: Gather the pieces that are left over. Let nothing be wasted.

Narrator: So the disciples gathered what was left. There were twelve full baskets full of fish and bread left over. It was indeed a miracle, which began with a little boy and his small snack.

~The End~

"Wow," said Iggy, smacking his lips. "Mrs. Holbrook, that was delicious. And just think! If that kid hadn't given his barley loaves and fish to Jesus, maybe all those people would have been like Logan here with a growling stomach."

"A very good point," said Mrs. Holbrook. "Just remember boys and girls, even if you don't think you have much to share, share whatever you have. God can multiply it and show His love to others with it."

Logan raised his hand. "Can I have more bread, please?"

"May I," corrected Mrs. Holbrook. "Sure. Cassie, would you pass the leftovers to Logan?"

Cassie did as her mom instructed. Several hands dove into the basket for seconds, including her own. After "Jesus" had fed the crowd in Sunday School, she was certain to be too full to eat later at the picnic.

Best Friends Forever?

10

After the worship service, J.J. and Cassie changed clothes in the ladies' room at the church. Cassie wished she and J.J. could just go and ride Chester all afternoon. She wanted to forget all about New Hope Center's picnic and especially Robyn. But it was clear that J.J. couldn't wait to see their new friend again.

"I'm going to take Robyn some of your mother's delicious bread," said J.J., showing Cassie the bread she had wrapped up and stored in her bag. "She will like that."

"My dad is probably waiting on us. We'd better hurry," said Cassie blandly. As the girls walked to Mr. Holbrook's pickup truck, it felt good to be in shorts for the afternoon. They climbed into the cab next to Mr. Holbrook and Iggy.

"Is Mom coming?" asked Cassie.

Mr. Holbrook slipped on his sunglasses and started the truck. "She's going home with Pat and Greta. I believe they made some last-minute plans this afternoon. You know, that picnic lunch sounds mighty good to me. I believe I'll stay for lunch, too."

Even before they got out of the truck, J.J., Cassie, and Iggy spotted Robyn on the front porch with two other children. Robyn seemed to be watching for them. As soon as Robyn saw the truck, she stood by on her crutches and waved excitedly. "Hey!" she yelled.

An older boy stood beside Robyn. He was clutching the hand of an adorable, tiny girl with chocolate-colored skin and bright pink beads threaded in her black, curly hair. The little girl was tugging at the boy's hand as she tried to coax him to run up and down the front steps with her.

Up the front steps of New Hope Center walked Cassie. J.J. and Iggy ran ahead. As they approached, Robyn wasted no time introducing her friends to each other. "Iggy, Cassie, and J.J., this is Hunter Harris and his little sister Madison."

"Oh," said J.J. "Is she your little tea party friend—the one you play with in your secret hiding place?"

"Right!" said Robyn. "Madison lost her hearing as a baby, so she has come to New Hope Center to learn sign language and receive hearing therapy. Hunter comes to see his little sister every weekend. We are very good friends."

"Hi," said Iggy, giving Hunter's free hand a friendly slap.

Best Friends Forever?

"Finally, another guy to hang with in the midst of all these girls. Now I won't feel so outnumbered."

"How's it going?" said Hunter, struggling to keep his balance. As little Madison pulled him up and down the steps, Hunter's closely shaven head bobbed about. "Hi Cassie, hi J.J. Anybody want a baby sister for the afternoon? Just kidding."

Everyone laughed at Hunter's joke. Cassie could tell that Hunter really loved his baby sister.

"Are you ready for a great picnic?" chirped Robyn. "The cooks have been whipping up a feast for days! I helped with the brownies."

"I can always eat," said Iggy, rubbing his tummy. "Let's go!"

They walked through the grass to the playground. J.J. turned cartwheels across the lawn, while Madison did somersaults. Iggy pulled out a small pocket camera and caught the action on film. The funniest shot was when Hunter did a somersault, too, and Madison leap-frogged over his head.

"J.J., will you teach me how to turn cartwheels like you when I get off these silly crutches?" Robyn asked.

"Oh sure, it's easy," said J.J., catching her breath. Her indigo eyes sparkled as she added, "You'll be flipping all over this place in no time."

In the open area between the playground and the flower garden, tables of food were covered with white sheets. The tables of food seemed to stretch for miles across the lawn. Cassie had never seen so much food in her life. Patients with their family members and friends were already lining up for Sunday dinner on the grounds.

"This looks a little like the Bible story scene we acted out in Sunday School," said J.J., "only the crowd in the Bible just had a boy's snack instead of a feast."

Robyn looked puzzled. "A boy's snack? To feed a big crowd? That's impossible!"

"Not for Jesus," said Iggy. "He turned a couple of little fish and a few small loaves of bread into enough to feed thousands of people and had twelve big baskets full left over!"

Robyn giggled. "That sounds like a really cool fairy tale," she said.

J.J. and Cassie looked at each other. They realized at the same time that Robyn didn't know about Jesus or the Bible!

Into Robyn's tiny hand, J.J. placed the package of bread she had brought from Sunday School. "Robyn," said J.J. "I used to think Bible stories were just fairy tales, too. But when I was younger, I learned some great news. Bible stories are not fairy tales. Bible stories are true, and Jesus Christ is God's Son. He can do anything, even multiply a little boy's lunch into enough food to feed thousands of people."

"Wow," said Robyn.

Hunter nodded. "That's right. I'm trying to tell my

little sister about Jesus. Since she's deaf, we can't 'talk' about Him. But my family and I show her pictures of Jesus helping people. She's real proud of the Bible we gave her for her birthday last year."

A glowing look of wonder came over Robyn's face. "Oh Hunter, does Madison have her Bible here at New Hope Center? I'd love to read it. You know, I've heard Aunt Felicia and Nurse Trixie say some nice things about Jesus."

Cassie remembered something. "There's a picture of Jesus with some children in the craft room. Have you noticed it?"

Robyn's eyes lit up. "Yes! When I was in a wheel-chair, Nurse Trixie would wheel me into the craft room. When I finished my craft project each after-noon, I would look up at that picture. I'd always imag-ine the nice man holding me in His lap with the other children in the picture. But I didn't know Jesus could perform miracles!"

"Yeah," said Iggy. "You can always count on Him. I haven't figured out everything about Jesus yet, but I know one thing. Jesus is the best friend anybody could ever have."

Just then, little Madison tugged Hunter's arm and pointed to the food. "Come on," said Hunter. "I think a certain someone is getting hungry!"

Everyone laughed and rushed to the end of the food line. Everyone except Cassie. She felt so ashamed of the selfish prayer that she had prayed in Sunday School that morning.

How could she have asked God to keep Robyn and J.J. apart during the picnic? Robyn needed to know Jesus, and J.J. was willing to tell her about Him. Cassie had never felt so horrible and selfish in her whole life. But she still didn't want to watch her best friend be pulled further away from her. Cassie simply could not bear to see J.J. growing closer to Robyn. She didn't know what to do.

While J.J. and Iggy slipped into line with Robyn, Hunter, and Madison, Cassie pretended that her shoe-strings needed retying. She sat in the grass and fumbled with the strings. Tears stung at her eyes, and she blinked them away. Suddenly, Cassie didn't want to be anywhere near the picnic. She wanted to be alone with her gloomy thoughts.

When no one was looking, she walked back across the lawn and slipped down the garden path that Robyn had shown them the day before. Past Robyn's secret hiding places she walked, head down. She could hear the crowd at the picnic laughing and talking. Cassie had never felt so alone in her entire life....

"*Quack!*"

Startled, Cassie looked up quickly. She realized she had walked all the way down the path to the petting zoo! As she opened the gate and stepped inside the fenced area, white ducks with orange bills waddled toward her, twitching their tail feathers. They seemed to be waiting for her to feed them. Cassie felt in her pockets for a crust of bread or something to give the ducks, but there was nothing to give them. The chickens happily pecked for their own food in the dirt.

"Shoo!" said Cassie to the ducks. "Go find your own food like the chickens!"

She sulked about until she found a shady spot under some towering pine trees. As she stared sullenly at the ground, someone in a big pair of familiar shoes approached. Cassie didn't have to look up to see that it was her dad. She would recognize those scuffed, brown leather shoes anywhere.

"Munchkin, I've been looking for you everywhere. Why aren't you in line? The rest of the children and their families are getting lunch. Just get a whiff of that barbecue! And I'm thirsty for a juicy bite of ice-cold watermelon. Come on. Let's get back to the picnic. I'm starved," he said cheerfully.

Cassie felt her father's broad, strong hand on her shoulder. Again, she had to fight back tears as she walked with him. But she refused to let a single tear roll down her cheek. She couldn't let Dad—or J.J.—know about her selfish thoughts and how much jealousy she felt towards Robyn. It was bad enough just realizing that God already knew all about what was burning in her heart.

She didn't want to lose her "best friend" friendship

with J.J. Yet somehow she had to make things right and stop feeling jealous of Robyn. But how?

Mr. Holbrook tightly squeezed his daughter in a bear hug, as they walked back toward the picnic tables. "You don't have to tell me what's wrong, but I know something is bothering you."

Cassie tried to smile, keeping her eyes down. "What makes you think something's wrong?" she asked.

"Oh, it doesn't take a rocket scientist to figure that out. With that forlorn look on your face, I can just about guess your conscience is bothering you. I know that look from raising your sisters."

Dad wasn't being judgmental. Cassie could hear the love in each word.

Cassie's fight against tears was getting tougher. She swallowed hard. "I've been thinking pretty selfishly, I guess. I didn't want to share my friend J.J. with Robyn, the girl on crutches ahead of us in line. I know I am wrong, but that is how I feel," said Cassie.

"Well now, it sounds like you're heading in the right direction," said her dad. "We all have selfish thoughts now and again. But that's easy to fix. We can admit to God when we are wrong and ask His forgiveness. Then He wipes the slate clean. God gives us another chance. We can start doing the right thing towards others."

"That's just it. What is the right thing?" asked Cassie. "I still don't want J.J. to stop being my best friend."

Best Friends Forever?

"Of course you don't," he said as he cupped her chin in his big hand and tilted her face up at his. Daddy's clear blue eyes met her hazel ones. "You can't choose someone else's friends for them. All you can do is try to be friendly with everyone you meet. You have a good heart, Cassie. I know you'll do the right thing. After you get your food, go sit with your friends. It might take time, but God will lead you. He will show you what to do," he said tenderly.

Cassie thought for a long moment. She wrapped her arms around her father and squeezed tightly. The tears behind her eyes began to dry up, and she smiled. She was still as confused as ever, but knowing that her dad believed she would do the right thing made her feel better.

As she went through the lunch line loading her plate with barbecue, chips, and carrot sticks, Cassie glanced across the grass at the circle of friends sitting beneath a gnarled oak tree. Cassie swallowed hard and tried to put on her brightest smile. Then she rejoined J.J., Robyn, Hunter, Iggy, and Madison. They sat in a circle with their plates piled high. Cassie scooted in beside J.J. and Iggy.

"Where have you been?" asked J.J. between bites.

Cassie tried to decide quickly what to say, without giving away her secret feelings. Should she tell them she had visited the chickens and ducks at the petting zoo?

Finally she smiled and replied, "I just 'ducked out' for a few minutes. What did I miss?" she asked.

"Iggy was telling us about his dreams of becoming a photojournalist," said Robyn, "and how he hopes to be part owner of his father's photography shop someday."

"That's awesome," said Hunter. "I want to fly jets like my Uncle Richard. He's an airline pilot out in California. He has routes to Japan and lots of faraway places. I think it would be exciting to see other countries. What do you think you would like to be when you grow up, J.J.?"

J.J. didn't have to think about her answer. "That's easy! I want to show horses professionally and be on the Olympic Equestrian team," she said. "All I have ever dreamed of is riding horses. I love anything and everything about horses. Someday I'll own a ranch and breed champion quarter horses."

"Oh," Robyn's aqua-blue eyes grew wide. "Horses are so romantic. I'm going to ride a horse someday, when I get off these silly crutches."

J.J. grabbed Cassie's arm. "I have the most wonderful idea! Cassie, you and I should take Robyn horseback riding when she is allowed!"

Robyn's mouth flew open in surprise. "Oh could I? Thank you, J.J.! Thank you, Cassie! That would mean so much to me! Boy, I hope Dr. Ken and Nurse Trixie will allow me to ride very soon," she said excitedly.

Best Friends Forever?

"What are friends for?" grinned J.J. "We'll have a great time. Won't we, Cass? Oh, we could show her Talking Rock and everything!" she said.

Cassie couldn't believe J.J. was inviting Robyn to Talking Rock! She couldn't find any words to speak. Life seemed out of control. All of a sudden, Robyn was being included in the activities that J.J. and Cassie had always shared.

Robyn reached over and took J.J.'s hand. "You don't know what it means to have new friends like all of you," she said, her eyes glowing. "I've been lonely in hospitals and sick beds forever. Now I have real friends. Hunter, Iggy, J.J., Cassie, you are all very special. You've given me something to look forward to—especially riding horses someday! Now I will work extra hard to get off these crutches during my physical therapy exercises. Wait and see. I will be strong and well again!"

Hunter signed the word for horse to Madison. Madison got up and "galloped" around the circle of friends. Everyone laughed except Cassie. The sad weight inside her heart just kept getting heavier.

For the rest of the afternoon, Cassie fought with herself to keep a cheerful attitude. She watched Robyn and J.J. continue to talk and play together. Cassie was starting to feel completely ignored. Iggy even seemed caught up in his new friendship with Hunter.

Adventures in Misty Falls

Cassie felt totally left out when Robyn and J.J. disappeared inside for a while. She tried not to feel jealous, but it wasn't working very well.

Best Friends Forever?

11

Finally, Cassie slipped over to speak to her dad. "Are you about ready to go home now? I need to check on Chester," Cassie whispered.

"I'm glad you said that," said Mr. Holbrook. "My easy chair is calling me home. It's time for my Sunday afternoon nap!"

What a relief! Cassie hopped into the truck first and watched J.J. hugging Robyn good-bye. Robyn looked toward the truck and waved. "Good-bye Cassie! Come back to see me!"

Cassie managed to wave and smile. She really did think Robyn was a nice girl. Those guilty, angry, and jealous feelings creeping around Cassie's heart were very upsetting.

On the way back to the farm, Mr. Holbrook dropped off Iggy and J.J. at their homes. Once Cassie arrived home, she couldn't wait to head for the barn. If there was one living being that could understand her at that moment, it was Chester.

She opened the barn door and walked across the long, open aisle to Chester's stall. Her pony peered over the stall at her as always. When she came close, she hugged and kissed his soft muzzle.

"Oh Chester," she said, finally letting a tear trickle down her cheek. "You are still my best buddy, aren't you?" Chester seemed to know that something was troubling Cassie. He nickered softly and played his "what's-in-your-pocket-to-eat?" game.

Suddenly, Cassie wanted to ride and never stop. She saddled and bridled her pony. In no time, off they went across the pasture, toward Possum Creek.

Chester was probably the best little trail-riding pony in Misty Falls. He was quite sure-footed on rocky hills and around tree roots. And as long as Cassie had a firm grip on the reins and the saddle horn, she wasn't even afraid to climb steep areas with her trusty little "pack horse."

What a relief to be alone with her pony! Cassie breathed in a big gulp of fresh country air and leaned over to pat Chester's neck as he trotted amiably along. Cassie let Chester follow his own beaten path through the pasture to Possum Creek. Then she steered him downstream along the creek bed. She loved the sound of water rippling over the rocks. As they made their way past the Holbrook family's favorite swimming hole in Possum Creek, she could hear the whooshing, tumbling roar of the waterfall in the distance. Cassie had never ridden all the way to the falls, except once with J.J.

Best Friends Forever?

Cassie tried not to think about J.J. and Robyn's growing friendship, but it was hard to forget how easily J.J. turned her attentions to Robyn and forgot about Cassie. Finally, Cassie said to Chester, "Oh buddy, if I don't stop thinking about this, I'll go stir-crazy!"

The creek took a crooked turn, and Cassie steered Chester around a thick patch of undergrowth. As she rejoined the creek on the other side of the bushes, there was a strangely familiar horse, drinking water in the clearing ahead.

The mare was red and sleek. No saddle, only a bridle. And her back was beautiful like that of a large deer. Cassie knew at once that it was Gracie.

Chester recognized Gracie too. His ears perked up high, and he nickered loudly. The pace of Chester's trot accelerated, as he hurried to her side. The animals nuzzled each other and "spoke" to each other in soft, low, throaty tones.

It was then that Cassie spotted J.J. sitting with her head down on a creek rock beside Gracie. "J.J.! What are you doing all the way over here?"

J.J. looked up. Her face was wet with tears. Cassie dismounted and ran to her friend's side. "What's wrong?" she whispered gently.

"Oh Cass, when I got home, my mom told me that a man wants to buy Gracie. She said that we can't afford to keep her any longer. I'm going to have to sell her right away! I can't bear to think of it!" said J.J. through her tears.

Horror struck Cassie like a bolt of lightning. "No! We can't let that happen. You can bring Gracie to our farm tonight and board her there at no charge. I'm sure my dad will agree."

"Do you think so, really?" said J.J hopefully. "Oh, but it's more than the boarding fees. My mom says we can't afford the expense of the veterinarian and Gracie's food and the entry fees and costumes for horse shows. A man has already named his price, and my mom wants to accept his offer. Oh Cassie, there goes my dream. What will I do without Gracie?"

Cassie's mind was suddenly spinning with bits and pieces of ideas. "We'll get jobs, and we'll earn the money to keep Gracie," she said in a determined stance.

"Don't you remember? I asked Mr. Phelps at the grocery store. No one will hire someone our age, at least until we are fourteen," said J.J.

"We can baby-sit," suggested Cassie.

"But baby-sitting isn't a steady job. I would need to earn quite a bit of money each week to keep Gracie," J.J. said as she broke into fresh sobs.

Cassie sat motionless with her arm around J.J.'s heaving shoulders.

There was only one thing to do. The girls would need to go straight to Cassie's father.

Best Friends Forever?

"Come on," said Cassie. "There's only one person I know who will understand."

"Who? Robyn?" J.J. asked.

Cassie shivered inside. Why would J.J. even think of Robyn at a time like this? "No, my father. Come on. Dad will help us figure this out."

Reluctantly, J.J. arose and slid onto Gracie's bare back. She followed Cassie back to the Holbrook farm, and they turned out the horses into the pasture to graze.

Once inside, Opie greeted the girls and gave J.J. her traditional doggy-lick bath. Then he pranced ahead of them to Mr. Holbrook's easy chair. Cassie's father had awakened from his afternoon nap and was reading the Sunday paper.

"Well, hello there, girls," he said, folding the sports page for a better view of his youngest son's football summer camp photo.

Mr. Holbrook noticed J.J.'s troubled expression on her face, but he didn't have a chance to ask any questions. Breathless, Cassie spilled out J.J.'s problem in one long, run-on sentence.

It went something like this…

"J.J.'s mother is having trouble paying their bills and Gracie is very expensive to keep because they have to board her and pay vet bills and food bills and J.J.'s horse show fees and costume expenses, and a man wants to buy Gracie and J.J.'s mom says she has no choice but to sell Gracie and J.J. simply can't sell Gracie, because Gracie is like a member of the family and J.J.'s dream is to compete in horse show events as a professional someday, maybe even the Olympics and J.J. needs a free place to board Gracie and a job to pay for Gracie's other expenses so that…"

"Hold it, hold it, hold it," said Mr. Holbrook with genuine concern. He laid down his paper and used his hand like a stop sign. "I think I've got the picture, Munchkin."

Cassie reached for J.J.'s hand. The girls sat frozen in place at Mr. Holbrook's feet, as he pondered the problem.

"That is quite a dilemma," said Mr. Holbrook. "It seems to me this is a problem for J.J. and her mother to work out. However, I do believe I know someone who would hire two young ladies like yourselves in exchange for room and board for a horse like Gracie."

"You do?" asked J.J. "Who?"

"Why, me, of course," said Mr. Holbrook with a grin. "A farmer always needs hired hands. But then again, I do work my helpers very hard, don't I, Munchkin?

"He sure does," giggled Cassie, rolling her hazel eyes. "Whew!"

"Oh, I don't mind," said J.J. "I don't mind hard work at all! And I will give up the horse show events for a while, if only I can keep Gracie."

Best Friends Forever?

Mr. Holbrook smiled. "See? There's the solution right there. Why don't you and I give your mother a call?" he asked.

"Oh would you, Mr. Holbrook?" J.J. asked. All of a sudden, J.J. stood up and gave Mr. Holbrook a kiss on the cheek. Then she turned beet-red. "Oh I'm sorry, Mr. Holbrook. Sometimes I wish I could have a father as nice as you. You are the nicest dad a girl could ever have."

"Well, I–uh, thank you J.J.," said Mr. Holbrook awkwardly.

"She's right, Dad," added Cassie. "You are the best."

"This is great!" said J.J, hugging Cassie. "I can't wait to email Robyn and tell her the good news!"

Cassie stared at J.J. She felt like she was staring at a stranger, certainly not J.J. Graystone, her best friend since first grade. "What do you mean by that?" Cassie asked.

"When my mom told me I was going to have to sell Gracie, I got on line with Robyn, and we talked about it for a while. She's such a sweet, understanding girl. I'm glad she's our friend, Cassie, aren't you?" J.J. said.

"No!" There. The word was out of Cassie's mouth. There was no holding back now. So Cassie blurted out the rest. "No, I'm not glad she's OUR friend. Besides, Robyn is *your* friend, *not mine!*"

With that, Cassie stumbled upstairs to her bedroom and closed the door. She threw herself on the bed and thrust her hands over her face. *What had she done? What had she said? How would she ever face J.J. again?*

Best Friends Forever?

12

Part of Cassie wanted to run right back down those stairs and apologize right away, but she wasn't sorry. She was angry and hurt and afraid of losing J.J. for good. She was also ashamed of herself. She wouldn't know what to say to J.J. after that awful outburst. Her feelings were out in the open now, for better or worse.

There was nothing to do but wait. Cassie sighed and looked out the window at Gracie and Chester grazing in the field. Their tails were swishing the flies off each other's faces. At least the horses were still good friends. As long as there was green grass to eat and flies to swish away, they would be the best of pals. She wished life was that simple for J.J. and her!

Just then a knock sounded at Cassie's door. "Who is it?" she asked.

"Me. J.J," she answered.

Cassie's heart jumped. She walked to the bedroom door and opened it.

"May I come in, Cass? We need to talk." J.J. said in a somber voice.

"Oh J.J.," Cassie cried, "It would serve me right if you never spoke to me again. I don't deserve a best friend."

"How can you say that?" J.J. began. Then the girls sat on Cassie's bed and looked out the window at their horses. "Cassie, you've made it possible for me to keep Gracie. I've already talked to my mom on the phone. Now she is talking to your dad, working out the details. I just can't thank you enough."

Cassie sighed. Her feelings began to melt away, and all that was left was a big desire to make things all right again with J.J.

"I'm sorry I blew up downstairs. We've never even had a little argument until today," said Cassie. "I guess I'm afraid that Robyn is becoming your new best friend and that you will forget about me."

J.J. looked like she had witnessed the landing of a UFO. "Are you kidding? How could anyone replace you? You are my best friend, Cassie. I thought you knew that I would never think of anyone else as my very best friend," said J.J.

"Oh J.J., I feel just awful. I'm so sorry I doubted you. I really don't want to feel jealous anymore," said Cassie. "If you want to be friends with Robyn, that's alright with me. I'll try to be friends with her, too. I just don't know how yet. I wasn't sure I wanted to share you with her, but now I see how silly that is."

"Oh Cass," said J.J., "Robyn has been through so much with that car accident and all those surgeries. She needs friends like us! But I think we need a friend like her twice as much!"

"You're right," said Cassie. "She's a very sweet girl. Look, I really want to make up for lost time. Why don't we ask Nurse Trixie to bring Robyn to my house within the next day or so. If she isn't up to horseback riding yet, we can at least groom the horses and show her the farm."

"That's a wonderful idea!" exclaimed J.J.

Just then, there was another knock at Cassie's door. Mr. Holbrook peeked inside. "Is the war over?" he asked, his eyes dancing.

The girls looked at each other and giggled. "Oh Dad," said Cassie, "yes, and I'm sorry for the way I acted."

"Well, I should hope so," he said with a wink. Then he turned to J.J. "Gracie can stay. It's all settled. And I expect two young ladies to report for duty in the barn at 7:30 A.M. sharp for work instructions!"

Cassie and J.J. hugged each other. "We'll be there!"

★★★★★★★★★★★★★★★★★

As soon as they got it arranged, Robyn came with Nurse Trixie to the Holbrook farm one day in the late afternoon. The weather was perfect—not too hot and not too humid. After a day of loading hay and grain into the barn, J.J. and Cassie's backs were sore, but they were cleaned up and waiting for Robyn in the driveway, ready to greet her when she arrived.

When Robyn got out of the car, she braced her weight against the crutches and hopped to the barn with them. "I can't wait to see the horses!" she exclaimed excitedly.

"Be careful, Robyn," called Nurse Trixie, running after them. "Horses are strong animals. You could get hurt by accident easily around horses."

"I'll be careful," Robyn yelled over her shoulder. It was clear that she was ready for adventure.

Gracie and Chester were in the big stall munching on a flake of hay. Robyn hobbled into the stall without fear, despite Trixie's warning.

Cassie reassured Trixie. "Don't worry. Chester wouldn't hurt a flea, and Gracie loves people," she said. "See? Chester is already nuzzling Robyn with his nose. That means he likes her."

"Oh, thank goodness," said Trixie. "We don't want any more setbacks for our young patient here. She has been through quite enough surgeries and hospital stays for a lifetime."

"I want to sit on Chester's back, please," said Robyn matter-of-factly.

"You what?" asked Trixie. "I don't know if that is such a good idea. How will you get up there?"

"Just for a while, please," said Robyn. "Someone will help me up."

"Now you wait just one minute, young lady!" said Trixie. "At least we need a saddle first."

Robyn clapped her hands. "Oh Trixie, you're the best!" she said. "Could I, Cassie?"

Cassie laughed aloud. Robyn was the spunkiest girl she had ever met. She was actually starting to like Robyn! "Sure," giggled Cassie, "if it's alright with your nurse, why would I mind?"

Cassie saddled Chester while J.J. bridled him. They walked him into the aisle of the barn where Cassie rode Chester on rainy days. Then Mr. Holbrook lifted Robyn carefully onto Chester's back. Robyn slid her feet into the stirrups and took a firm hold of the reins, just like a professional rider.

"I've seen the horse shows on television, so I know how to ride," said Robyn.

Cassie smiled. "You look great up there, Robyn! Now cluck to him, and he will walk forward for you," she said.

Robyn made a clucking noise with her tongue. Chester's ears perked up, and he ambled slowly around the barn.

"Oh, this is so much fun! Faster, Chester, faster!" exclaimed Robyn with glee.

Chester kept moving at the same slow pace as before. Then Robyn clucked to him again. Chester began to pick up the pace, just a bit faster. Robyn bounced in the saddle, but she held on tight. "Good pony! Yee-hah!" she shouted.

"Hey," said Cassie cheerfully, "I think Chester obeys you better than he obeys me!"

After Nurse Trixie saw what a good rider Robyn was, she allowed Cassie to walk Robyn and Chester out of the barn and into the pasture. "Bring her back soon," called Trixie. "I'm waiting right here, and I'd better not have to come looking for you young ladies."

"We'll be back soon," said Cassie.

Cassie walked with Chester, holding his head. Riding Gracie, J.J. followed Chester and Robyn. Cassie watched ever so carefully to make sure Chester would not step in a hole in the pasture. She didn't want Robyn to fall off and hurt herself.

The three girls and two horses walked all the way to Possum Creek and back. Robyn squealed with delight as Chester pranced through the green grass. J.J. and Cassie pointed out Talking Rock to Robyn.

"Next time you come to the farm, we will go out and sit on Talking Rock," said Cassie.

"Wow," said Robyn. "I can't wait!"

Next, the older girls showed Robyn the old barn where they played basketball with Iggy. "When you come back," said J.J., "Would you like to go against Iggy and Hunter in a game of basketball?"

Best Friends Forever?

"Would I ever!" exclaimed Robyn, patting Chester's neck. That half-hour pony ride had put sunshine in Robyn's smile like never before.

Afterward, the girls groomed the horses so well that the animals glistened in the light of the setting sun. J.J., Robyn, and Cassie turned out Chester and Gracie for their evening meal in the pasture.

Meanwhile, Trixie and Mrs. Holbrook set out the picnic supplies on the porch. Mr. Holbrook built a campfire. Cassie, J.J., and Robyn called Hunter and Iggy to join them for a wiener roast. While they were waiting for the boys to arrive, Cassie's older brothers and sisters joined them for a tournament of checkers on the porch. Robyn and Jeff emerged as the checkers champions.

Later, the whole family came out to enjoy hot dogs and roast marshmallows. They also made s'mores with the marshmallows, bits of chocolate bars, and graham crackers.

"Hey!" Iggy complained, as a marshmallow slid off his roasting stick. "My marshmallows keep melting and falling into the fire."

Cassie giggled. "Silly, don't hold your marshmallow IN the fire. Hold it above the fire. Then it won't melt and fall off and burn up."

The girls looked at each other and giggled. "Here, let us roast them for you," suggested Cassie.

Meanwhile, Iggy took pictures of the gang around

the campfire. He paused to gobble each marshmallow as it became perfectly toasted.

Mrs. Holbrook began to clean up the food on the porch. "Does anyone want another hot dog or chips or more baked beans or potato salad?" she asked.

The whole crowd groaned. "We're so full. We couldn't eat another bite," said Hunter. "Thank you, Mrs. Holbrook."

"You're welcome," laughed Cassie's mother. "It was quite a feast—like the day Jesus fed the crowd fish and barley loaves of bread. I didn't think we would have enough for such a hungry group. But we had more than plenty of food, after all," she said.

Cassie turned to Robyn and gave her a hug. "Robyn, I'm glad you came out to our farm today. I'm so happy you enjoyed your first ride on Chester. You can ride him anytime you want."

"Really?" asked Robyn. "It's a dream come true. Thank you so much, Cassie. I'm glad you and J.J. are my friends."

"Me, too," said Cassie. "And I'm glad you are our friend, too."

Cassie sighed and gazed at the crescent moon that rose in the sky. She realized that night that God had done a little miracle in her heart. It wasn't a big miracle, such as when Jesus fed thousands of people with a little boy's lunch, but it was a miracle just the same.

Best Friends Forever?

Cassie knew that God had taken the love in her heart and multiplied it. Suddenly, there was enough love for all of Cassie's friends—the old ones and the new ones—with twelve baskets full of love left over.

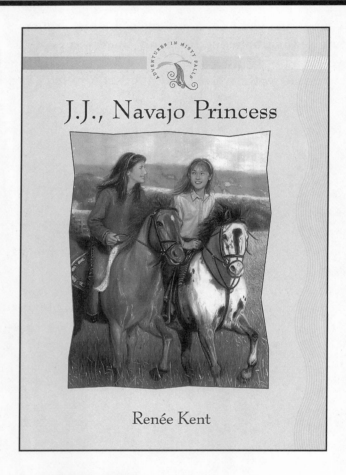

J.J., Navajo Princess
1-56309-763-X
N007105
$4.99

J.J., NAVAJO PRINCESS

RENÉE KENT

Condensed Excerpt from *J.J., Navajo Princess*

Joy bubbled within J.J. Graystone and spilled over into her clear, indigo eyes. Without a doubt, riding bareback was J.J.'s favorite way to travel, especially at the Holbrook family's farm on the outskirts of Misty Falls. The huge farm was a perfect place to ride for hours on end.

"Watch this, Cass," she said. First, she closed her eyes. Then she flung out her arms freely in the air. In a spirit of victory, she proclaimed, "See? I'm Nascha, a Navajo princess. Nascha is Grandmother Teresa's name for me."

Cassie gasped. "Princess or no princess! Jennifer Joy Graystone, you stop that! You're scaring me to pieces!" But J.J. only laughed. Making Cassie squirm was such fun!

"Sorry, Cass!" J.J. said. "Don't be alarmed. I just feel so, so...free!"

That free feeling came anytime she was riding Gracie. She always loved pretending that she was back on the Navajo Reservation with Grandmother Teresa. Even though J.J. only remembered a few Navajo words, and Grandmother only knew a few English words, they understood each other's hearts very well.

Most of the time, J.J. felt glad to live in Misty Falls. After all, she had the best friends ever—Cassie, Iggy, and her new friends Robyn and Hunter. Still, she missed Grandmother.

"Are you thinking about Grandmother Teresa again?" Cassie asked. Cassie always seemed to know what J.J. was thinking.

J.J. smiled. "You know me very well," she said. "When I was very young girl and living on the Navajo Reservation, I sometimes stayed with my grandmother in the old hogan. When Mom and I moved to Misty Falls, I cried for Grandmother every night. Even now, I still sometimes dream I am with her in the canyon, tending sheep or selling turquoise jewelry to the tourists."

An evening breeze began to softly freshen the girls' moist, hot faces. Even the horses seemed to enjoy the breeze, since the flies couldn't light on their faces. For a long moment, the girls fell silent. A whippoorwill moaned his sad birdcall from a distant tree branch across the pasture.

Cassie spoke first. "Are you sorry that you moved here to Misty Falls?"

J.J. studied her friend's concerned hazel eyes. "Oh, Cass, you know how much I love living here in Georgia with you. It is just so far away from my clan. You know, my family. Aunts, uncles, cousins, and Grandmother Teresa. I was five when I left the Navajo Reservation. I can't remember many of the family members that my mother talks about. I would like to know them. But most of all, I miss my grandmother."

"I don't blame you," said Cassie, stroking Chester's neck. "My whole family lives here in Misty Falls. I can't imagine living far away from them."

"You understand everything," J.J. said gratefully. "See? If God really does work everything out for the best for those who love Him, He must have moved me here, so that we could be best friends."

The horses with their two riders flat-walked toward the creek to the girls' private talking spot, Talking Rock.

"You must have felt very sad leaving your grandmother," said Cassie.

J.J. replied softly. "I still write

to her every week. Before we send it, Mom has to translate it into the Navajo language."

"Does she write back?" asked Cassie hopefully.

"Yes. She sends me tiny dried flowers from the canyon. Mom translates her letters for me. I know some Navajo words, but I can't remember many. It's a very difficult language."

Cassie thought and thought. Finally she said, "Why don't you go for a visit to the Navajo Reservation? There's still a little time before school starts. You could see your grandmother and all your clan."

"I asked my mom at the beginning of summer, but she says we can't afford the trip. Besides, a visit is just a visit. It will not be the same as living there. Mother worries about Grandmother Teresa now that she is getting older. If only my grandmother and I were together...."

Cassie thought for a moment. Then her face brightened. "You know, Dad is talking about taking our family out west next summer. Maybe you could come, too!"

"That would be great!" said J.J. She felt like smiling and crying at the same time. "But that is still a whole year away. Oh, Cassie, do you really think I could go with you and your family? Who would take care of the farm? Who would take care of Gracie and Chester?"

"I don't know. But if we start praying now, God will have lots of time to work it out," said Cassie. "Don't worry."

"Let's pray right now," said J.J., feeling hopeful. She didn't know quite what to ask for. So sitting with their legs criss-crossed on Talking Rock, the girls held hands, bowed their heads, and began to have a conversation with God. J.J. liked how Cassie talked directly to Jesus Christ. Cassie asked God for his help in making J.J.'s dream come true.

But J.J. wasn't sure exactly what her dream was. She just knew that she missed her grandmother, and that the ache in her heart wouldn't go away.

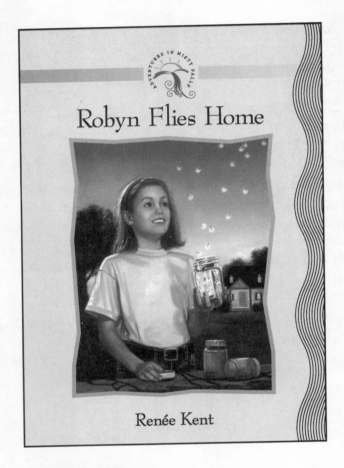

Robyn Flies Home
1-56309-764-8
N007106
$4.99

Address: ▼ http://www.mistyfallsfriends.com

Back Forward Stop Refresh Home Search Mail Favorites

A WHOLE NEW MISTY FALLS WORLD IS READY FOR YOU TO EXPLORE ON THE WEB!

What do Cassie, J.J., and the gang
do in their spare time?

What games do they like to play?

What does Misty Falls look like?

**Visit
www.mistyfallsfriends.com
to find out!**

Don't miss any of the adventures of Cassie and the Misty Falls gang.

Read all the books!

Cassie, You're a Winner!
1-56309-735-4
N007116
$4.99 retail price
$1.99 through 12/31/00

Best Friends Forever?
1-56309-734-6
N007117
$4.99

J.J., Navajo Princess
1-56309-763-X
N007105
$4.99

Robyn Flies Home
1-56309-764-8
N007106
$4.99

Look for books 5 and 6—available in October 2000!